"Yes, Mr. Bartlett, I Can Find You A Wife...

"But you're going to have to cooperate...give up some of your unrealistic expectations and put yourself completely in my hands."

Shane blinked, taken aback by Cassie's tone. "What do you mean, 'unrealistic expectations'?"

Cassie leaned forward earnestly, ignoring him. "You've got to trust me completely. From this moment on, I'm going to be your shadow. You're going to tell me things you wouldn't tell your priest, and you're going to listen to me when I tell you what to do. As of this very minute, you're turning yourself completely over to me, is that understood?"

There was a fervor in her eyes that overwhelmed Shane. He wasn't sure he liked being told what to do by a woman. Then again, he had to give her credit for knowing her business, and there were surely worse things than putting himself in the hands of a woman who looked as pretty as she did.

Dear Reader:

Sensual, compelling, emotional...these words all describe Silhouette Desire. If this is your first Desire, let me extend an invitation for you to sit back, kick off your shoes and enjoy. If you are a regular reader, you already know what awaits you—a wonderful love story!

A Silhouette Desire can encompass many varying moods and tones. The books can be deeply moving and dramatic, or charming and lighthearted. But no matter what, each and every one is a terrific romance written by and for today's women.

I know you'll love March's *Man of the Month*, *Rule Breaker* by Barbara Boswell. I'm very pleased and excited that Barbara is making her Silhouette Books debut with this sexy, tantalizing romance.

Naturally, I think *all* the March books are outstanding. So give into Desire...you'll be glad that you did!

All the best,

Lucia Macro
Senior Editor

DONNA
CARLISLE

MATCHMAKER,
MATCHMAKER

SILHOUETTE *Desire*

Published by Silhouette Books New York

America's Publisher of Contemporary Romance

SILHOUETTE BOOKS
300 East 42nd St., New York, N.Y. 10017

ISBN: 0-373-05555-2

First Silhouette Books printing March 1990

Printed in the U.S.A.

Books by Donna Carlisle

Silhouette Desire

Under Cover #417
A Man Around the House #476
Interlude #530
Matchmaker, Matchmaker #555

DONNA CARLISLE

lives in Atlanta, Georgia, with her teenage daughter.
Weekends and summers are spent in her rustic north
Georgia cabin, where she enjoys hiking, painting and
planning her next novel.

Donna has also written under the pseudonyms
Rebecca Flanders and Leigh Bristol.

One

Shane Bartlett spent a moment studying the dark-paneled office door, but the discreet gold numbers told him nothing except that he had found the right address. Behind that door could have been anything from a dentist's office to a high-priced brothel. He pushed open the door cautiously, fully prepared to bolt if he didn't like what he saw.

One brief glance around reassured him somewhat. The walls were covered with a dark blue floral print and hung with snapshots of wedding couples and babies. The carpet was a soothing light blue and the sofas were covered in a matching print. There were many small tables, also crowded with framed photographs, and a silver tea service in one corner. The only sign that this was a place of business was a small desk with curved

legs, which was set against a window, and it was empty.
Shane could have been walking into his grandmother's parlor—if he had a grandmother and if she had a
parlor. The entire effect was homey and welcoming,
designed to put a visitor at ease, and Shane relaxed as
he came inside and closed the door behind him. A soft
chime announced his arrival.

He looked around for a moment, wondering what he
was supposed to do now, and finally decided he was
expected to take a seat on one of the miniature sofas
and wait. There was no one else waiting but him, which
was another thing he liked—discretion, as in a psychiatrist's office where appointments were scheduled so
that one patient wouldn't meet another in the waiting
room. Not, of course, that Shane Bartlett had ever
been in a psychiatrist's office, any more than he had
ever been in a place like this.

He started to feel uneasy again as he pushed his
Stetson back on his head and lowered his long frame
onto the sofa. He tried leaning back, crossing one
booted ankle over his knee, then sat forward again on
the edge of the sofa. The room was too quiet, and too
small. The silence he could tolerate; he had known a lot
of that. But he still wasn't used to being under a real
roof, and everything in Dallas was much smaller than
he had been led to believe.

An inner door opened, and Shane sprang to his feet
as a plump, matronly-looking woman came through.
Her hair was gray, her dress was a flower-printed silk
and her smile was warm. "You must be Mr. Bartlett,"
she said.

He quickly swept off his hat, embarrassed that he hadn't thought to do it before. He had been living with men too long; it was obvious his manners needed a little polishing. "Yes, ma'am," he said. "I called."

She extended a plump, soft hand. "I'm Emma Humphrey. I'm sorry to keep you waiting."

The last of Shane's doubts disappeared as he took the woman's hand. Even her name sounded as if it belonged to someone's mother, and she smelled of lavender. This might not be so bad, after all.

She went behind the desk and picked up a clipboard with several papers on it. "We have a questionnaire we'd like you to fill out. Everything is confidential, I assure you. If you'll just have a seat..."

Shane took the clipboard and flipped through the papers dubiously. Twelve pages, small print. He looked back at her. "Ma'am," he said, "I once went to an army recruiting office. They handed me a bunch of papers like this to fill out. I always did think the army missed a hell of a deal."

He handed the clipboard to her, and her expression was puzzled. "I'm not much for writing things down," he said by way of explanation. "The way I figure it, life's too short. Couldn't we just talk about this?"

She hesitated. "Well, it really isn't routine...." Then she smiled, seeming to sense his discomfort, and picked up the telephone. "Perhaps in your case we can put the interview first. Let me see if Miss Averil has time to see you now."

He was dismayed. "You mean there's another one? I thought you—"

She smiled and spoke into the receiver. "Cassie, Mr. Bartlett is here. Yes, but he wanted to talk to you first."

There was silence, during which Shane considered abandoning the entire project. This thing was quickly getting more complicated than he had counted on. Explaining the situation to this sweet, motherly-looking woman was one thing, but trying to impress a complete stranger.... Shane was beginning to think he would have been better off taking out an ad in the paper.

After a moment, Emma replaced the telephone and smiled at him again, indicating the door through which she had recently entered. "Just go right in. Miss Averil will be glad to talk to you."

From the part of the conversation he had heard, Shane doubted that, but he followed her instructions, anyway. The minute he opened the door to the inner office, his misgivings were confirmed.

Cassie Averil was not only young, she was pretty, too... or almost pretty. Of course, Shane had been in the wilderness for so long that anything that didn't wear horseshoes or bite would look pretty to him, so he didn't entirely trust his own judgment. Her hair, a rich dark auburn, was pulled back from her face in a tight bun. She wore huge tortoiseshell glasses which, by accident or design, picked up the coppery highlights in her hair. Her skin was fair, her cheekbones rounded, her mouth a little too wide. She was wearing a dark suit and a stiff-collared white blouse, and when she stood up Shane immediately revised his first impression. She had almost no hips, and very little up front to speak of. That was disappointing.

She extended her hand. "Mr. Bartlett, I'm Cassandra Averil. It's a pleasure to meet you."

She had a honey-smooth Southern drawl, which Shane liked. But her handclasp was cool, and so was her voice. Despite the drawl, Shane decided he had seen dozens of girls in Dallas who were prettier than she was, and they didn't bother to hide it behind men's suits and tortoiseshell glasses. He began to feel marginally more comfortable.

"Please, have a seat." She indicated the green brocade chair drawn up in front of her desk. "What can I do for you?"

Shane decided right there that there was nothing to do but plunge right in. He had come too far to back down now.

He sat down, crossed his ankle over his knee, and said, "You can find me a woman."

Cassie kept her face expressionless. She looked him over carefully, from his curly hair to the well-worn bottoms of his dusty cowboy boots, and idly wondered what century he was from. His coloring was in shades of a Texas sandstorm—light brown hair, deep brown eyes, coppery brown skin. His stamped leather vest was expensive, the jeans and shirt ordinary, the silver belt buckle garish. The hat was too much, and the boots—well, they *did* look as though they had come from another century, and had walked clear through to this one.

He was good-looking enough, with a firm jaw and a slight shading that suggested five-o'clock shadow, lips that were full without being too sensual, and a frank, well-set gaze. His nose was a little big. He was tall, close to six-four, unless she missed her guess, but he didn't stoop the way a lot of tall men did. He had strong, straight shoulders and he bore them with natural grace, which was a pleasant change from men who spent five days a week at the gym developing biceps and trapeziuses, and then walked as though they were carrying a balancing board across their shoulders. His handclasp had been strong and work-roughened, and she knew those shoulder muscles hadn't come from lifting weights. He had long, lean thighs, and not one ounce of spare flesh curled over that gaudy belt buckle. Taken piece by piece, he was an attractive man, and there were a lot of women who liked the rugged cowboy type. Cassie wasn't one of them.

Under other circumstances she would have been more charitable, but she had had a rotten day and the last thing she needed at the end of it was for some overconfident caveman to come strolling into her office and demand that she "find him a woman." It was the kind of thing that made her wonder, more and more, why she had ever gotten into this business.

As her silence lengthened, Shane asked a little anxiously, "That is what you do, isn't it? Find women?"

Cassie took a small breath. "We are not an escort service, Mr. Bartlett."

"Good." He relaxed again. "Because I'm not looking for an escort. I'm looking for a wife."

Once again Cassie managed to hide her reaction. This man ordered a wife as easily as he would have ordered a steak, medium rare, extra potatoes and hold the sour cream. She went on, "We make social introductions based on probable compatibility for the purpose of companionship and, hopefully, romance. Naturally we're always happy when our introductions lead to long-term relationships, but I'm sure you understand that we make no guarantees.''

Shane stared at her for a moment. He couldn't remember the last time he had heard anyone use so many words to say so little. He jerked a thumb toward the door. ''You call yourself Matchmakers, Inc., right? All those pictures on the wall outside—they're of people you got married, aren't they? Well, that's what I'm here for. To get married.''

This time Cassie couldn't help it; she stared at him. *This man cannot be for real,* she thought. She started to make a mental list of all the people she knew who might consider this kind of practical joke funny, but the man sitting opposite her looked perfectly sincere. And why not? After the kind of day she had had, why in the world not?

She cleared her throat and picked up her pen. ''Well, I must say it's refreshing to meet someone who knows what he wants,'' she murmured.

''That's the only way to get anywhere in this world,'' he replied confidently. ''Make up your mind what you want and then go for it.''

Cassie tapped her pen absently against her notepad, still examining him carefully for some sign of a joke. He gave none. ''Well,'' she said abruptly. ''Why don't you start by telling me something about yourself?''

He seemed a bit skeptical. ''Like what?''

''Like how old you are, what you do for a living...''

"Oh." He leaned back and rested his elbows on the narrow arms of the chair, which seemed too small for him. The checked material of his shirt tightened nicely across his chest as he did so.

"I'm thirty-two years old, and I've spent the past fifteen of those years working on the pipeline in Alaska. Now I don't do much of anything if I can help it."

She lifted an eyebrow. "Retired?"

"Well, I'm not saying I'm a multimillionaire, but I've done okay for myself. I'm well able to support a wife, if that's what you're asking."

"I see." This was getting more interesting by the minute. It could still be a joke, but . . .

"I don't mean to rush you, but I've got some things I'd like to do this afternoon, so why don't I just tell you what I'm looking for and you can get to work?"

"I'm afraid it's a little more complicated than that, Mr. Bartlett."

He waved a dismissing hand. "Nothing's complicated unless you make it. Do you have any pictures or videotapes or anything like that I can look at?"

"This is not a police station, Mr. Bartlett," Cassie replied coolly. "We do not keep mug shots. This is a highly exclusive, personalized service and our clients respect our discretion just as much as we respect their privacy."

The import of her speech was lost on him as he lifted one shoulder in a shrug. "Well, it doesn't matter. You just take notes and I'll tell you what to look for. First of all, I like blondes. Natural blondes. About twenty, twenty-two—"

"We often find," Cassie interrupted firmly, "that a large age difference isn't conducive to compatibility. Perhaps you should consider—"

"I expect to have lots of kids," he said, as though that explained everything.

Cassie's hand tightened on the pen.

"Not too small," he went on. "I don't like bending over when I'm looking at a woman. And a little on the fleshy side, if you know what I mean. Hips and bosoms, you know."

Cassie kept her tone civil with difficulty. This man was really too much. "Shall we say a size thirty-six C?"

He had the grace to look uncomfortable. "I don't know too much about sizes, but that sounds about right." He cleared his throat and went on more confidently. "I like long hair, too, and not too much makeup. Kind of natural-looking."

Cassie smiled tightly. "The natural look is sometimes hard to find in a wind-up doll."

"Well, I'm not saying she has to be be perfect. Not a beauty queen, or anything. But pretty. No sense pretending I don't like pretty women, is there?"

"No, not at all." Cassie leaned back and spread her hands expansively. "I want you to be perfectly frank about what you like. How else will we be able to please you? Now, so far we have a twenty-year-old blond with long hair and thirty-six C cups who's into childbearing and isn't too short. Anything else?"

But her sarcasm was lost on him as he answered, "Well, she shouldn't talk too much. She should like to cook, and bake—pies and cakes especially. And she should like to do things for a man, you know? Little things, like running his bath and making him a drink without his asking for it. I guess it should go without saying that she shouldn't have a roving eye. And don't give me any of these career types. I want a woman who likes to make a home for a man and be there for him."

Cassie kept her eyes on her notepad, where she was making sharp, geometric doodles. "I assume she should be free of disease and have good teeth?"

For the first time he sounded a little taken aback. "Now don't get me wrong. I know this isn't a mail-order catalog or anything."

She looked up at him. "Neither is it an à la carte restaurant. We don't keep models on the back shelves just waiting for someone to come in and place an order." She didn't know why she was letting him get to her; another time she would have been amused. But after the accumulated tensions of the day, an encounter with a world-class chauvinist was the last straw. Her voice rose a little as she said, "Let me ask you something, Mr. Bartlett. This woman you're looking for— is it all right if she thinks occasionally? And if she's read one or two books in her life, do you disqualify her?"

He frowned. "Of course not. I mean, yeah, sure I want her to think. What I'm trying to say is—"

"And I suppose you want her to be a virgin, too?"

She actually thought he flushed. "Well, I didn't say that, but—"

"And maybe if she's a good girl in between kids, you might take her for a ride in the car with the top down."

He shuffled in his seat. "Now listen, Miss—"

"Ms.," Cassie corrected tightly.

He looked uncertain. "Listen, maybe I'm going about this the wrong way, but it just seemed to me it would be easier all the way around if I told you what kind of woman I'm looking for. I don't know what I did to make you mad, but I thought this was the kind of thing you did. If it's not, just say so."

Cassie took a deep breath and stood slowly, bracing her palms against the desk. "Mr. Bartlett," she said, very calmly, "as I've tried to explain to you before, what we do at Matchmakers is to introduce compatible people to each other. Our clientele is largely composed of earnest, sincere business people who are genuinely looking for a relationship but lack the time or social contacts to form one in the more conventional fashion. We cannot manufacture wives, or life-size dolls, for that matter. As for you..." She took another deep breath. "May I suggest you go out and find yourself a nice dog? A dog is loyal, obedient, doesn't talk too much, and will even fetch your slippers at night. I'm afraid there's nothing we can do for you here at Matchmakers. Good day."

After a moment Shane Bartlett picked up his hat and stood. He paused at the door and looked back with a puzzled expression on his face, and Cassie thought he would say more. But he apparently changed his mind and left the office without another word.

When he was gone, Cassie sank back into her chair and blew out her breath through her teeth. She couldn't believe she had just talked to a potential client that way. She couldn't believe that with the rent ten days overdue and Final Notice stamped all over the telephone bill that she had just thrown a paying customer out of her

office. She had been in this business too long; it was
beginning to affect her nerves and judgment.

The door opened and Emma poked her head in.
"Well, that was quick."

Cassie looked up at her. "Tell me something, Emma.
If a perfectly healthy, reasonably attractive-looking
man walked in here demanding that you find a twenty-
year-old blonde with C cups to bear his children, what
would you do?"

"If I were thirty years younger, I'd dye my hair and
marry him. What did you do?"

"Threw him out."

"Not a wise move." Emma handed her an opened
letter. "They're coming for the furniture on Monday."

Cassie groaned out loud, pushed her glasses up onto
her forehead and pressed her palms against her eyes.
"Doesn't matter," she muttered after a moment, her
voice muffled by her hands. "He didn't look as if he
could afford our fee, anyway."

"Wrong again." Emma sat down in the chair that
Shane had just vacated, and Cassie looked up at her
with more than a little trepidation. "Jack Sanders just
called," Emma explained. "Seems he's the one who
recommended your services to the young man in question. Jack is his architect, and Mr. Bartlett just bought
the Long Acre property. He just wanted to make sure
his friend got a proper introduction."

Cassie took a moment to let the information sink in.
The Long Acre property *and* the most sought-after—
and expensive—architect in town. Shane Bartlett might

be a nut, but he was a serious nut. With money. "Well," she said dully, "I guess I blew it."

Emma was tactfully silent.

Cassie looked around the elegantly furnished little room and no longer bothered to keep the despair out of her eyes. "I never should have moved the office. You tried to tell me. But, oh, no, I had to have an expensive address...."

"Now you hush," Emma said sternly. "I'm just an old woman who doesn't like change and you were right not to pay me any mind. This swanky uptown address is just what you need for all those fancy-pants oil-men."

"Who never come." Cassie's smile was wan. She slid down in her chair until she could rest her head against the back and lace her fingers across her stomach. "Let's face it, Emma. In less than a year I've managed to destroy what it took my mother a lifetime to build."

"Stop talking that nonsense. You—"

But Cassie shook her head firmly and got to her feet. "No, I was wrong from the beginning and I should have seen it coming."

She moved restlessly over to the window, parted the blinds and looked out over the busy Dallas street. "Nobody needs a matchmaking service anymore. When Mother was doing it people cared about finding the perfect mate—with the right background, common interests, a compatible personality—the things you build a marriage on. They wanted catered dinners, gifts from Tiffany's, three-piece orchestras and moonlight sails to a private island. But why should they pay for our kind of personalized service when they can call up a dating club and flip through cutesy videotapes for half the price? Who cares about forming a meaningful relationship when all you have to do is dial a 900 number to trade sex fantasies with a member of the opposite sex? My mistake was in taking this whole business seriously. And what do I get for my trouble? Somebody like this Shane Bartlett who comes strolling in here expecting me to pull his favorite fantasy right out of a filing cabinet.''

"Oh, I don't know," murmured Emma. "Wasn't it you who said that romance was a science, not an art? The right mixture of ingredients in the right amounts, a fail-safe formula, I believe you said."

Cassie frowned a little, feeling trapped by her own words. "That's just the point," she said. "It *is* a formula, and like everything in science, each step has to be followed precisely, logically and by somebody who knows what she's doing. If people would just leave me alone and let me do my job, I could guarantee one hundred percent success every time. But these people who come in here with preconceived notions about what will make them happy..."

"The very nerve," observed Emma with a twinkle in her eye.

Cassie scowled more deeply. "You know perfectly well what I'm talking about. People like that cowboy who just walked out of here, expecting his dream girl to come wrapped in cellophane and expecting *me* to wave a magic wand and produce her. Well, there is no magic." Her voice grew more fervent as she warmed up to her favorite subject. "That's the whole trouble with people today—they expect too much. Bells are supposed to ring and doves are supposed to fly and rose petals are supposed to fall from the sky, and if you give them anything else, they don't believe it's real. If people would just put aside their fantasies for one minute and realize that forming a relationship is no more complicated than baking a cake, they'd be a lot happier."

"And you'd be out of business."

That drew a rueful smile from Cassie. "Yeah, I guess I would." She looked at Emma intently. "I *am* good, aren't I? I mean, I have satisfied customers, haven't I? I know you don't always agree with my philosophy, but I *do* fulfill a need, and I keep them coming back." She saw the expression in Emma's eyes and lifted a defensive hand. "Oh, I know in my mother's day repeat customers weren't a measure of success, but that's not my fault. No one wants to get married anymore. I give people what they want, and what they want is an easy relationship."

"Mr. Bartlett does," Emma commented.

"Does what?"

"Wants to get married."

"Oh, him." Cassie waved a hand dismissively, bristling at the mere memory of the encounter. "He didn't want a wife. He wanted a windup doll. Well, I wish him all the luck in the world. With an attitude like that he's going to need it."

"Still, it's a pity. Finding him a wife would have given you a chance to prove your theory."

Cassie took off her glasses, rubbed the bridge of her nose and looked at Emma curiously. The glasses were

heavy and made her head hurt, but typical of everything else that had gone wrong lately, Cassie had de-
veloped an allergy to her contact lens solution and
would be forced to wear glasses for at least a couple of
weeks. "What do you mean?"

"What you're always saying," Emma replied inno-
cently. "That there's someone for everyone and all it
takes is the right scientific—" she emphasized the word
slightly "—method to find it."

Cassie made a face. "Well, he would have been a
challenge, all right." Then she looked at Emma suspiciously. "You really don't think I know what I'm
doing, do you?"

Emma smiled gently and got to her feet. "I think
you're very good at what you do," she assured her.
"It's just that all your data files and probability curves
and compatibility charts seem a little dry to me. Maybe
I still believe in the power of good old-fashioned romance. And—" she lifted an admonishing finger
"—it might not hurt you to give it a try, either."

Cassie opened her mouth for a rebuttal, but it was an
old disagreement that led nowhere. Emma had worked
for her mother and now she worked for Cassie, and she
hadn't made the transition between the generations
very easily. After a moment Cassie merely shrugged.
"Well, it doesn't matter. The probability curve on
finding Shane Bartlett a match drops off the chart—
with or without that mythological thing you call romance. And I'm glad I kicked him out," she decided
firmly. "A person's got to draw the line somewhere.
Although—" her tone grew thoughtful as she was

forced to admit honestly "—if I had it to do over again, I'd get his deposit first."

Emma chuckled, came over and slid her arm around Cassie's shoulders in a brief hug. "You go home," she said, "and have a nice bubble bath and a cup of tea. Things will look better tomorrow."

"The overdue bills will still be here," Cassie said glumly.

"True," agreed Emma cheerfully. "But by then we'll have figured out a way to pay them. We always do."

Emma went to close up the office, and after a moment Cassie gave a resigned lift of her shoulders and locked up her desk. She didn't really think anything would get better with a night's sleep, but there was no point in sitting around the office waiting for the phone to ring. She picked up her purse and started for home, where she could spend the evening looking at her own unpaid telephone bill and overdue rent notice while trying to figure out some way to turn things around.

As Emma had said, she always did.

Shane walked with his hands in his pockets, his head down and his stride long and angry. He felt like a fool. He had known it was a stupid idea to go to a place like that, and now he had not only wasted his time but had been soundly humiliated in the process. Matchmakers, indeed. He should have known nothing would be that easy.

He stopped by his red Corvette, put his hand on the door handle, then hesitated. Somehow the sight of the gleaming car took the edge off his temper, and as he ran his hand along the flawless finish, his dark mood softened. There were racier models, he knew, and more expensive ones, and he could have had his pick of any of them. But years ago, when he had first started working on the line and leaves were few and far between, he had gotten his hands on a rare copy of a stateside magazine and had seen an advertisement for a red Corvette. He had torn the picture out of the magazine and had carried it around until it had literally fallen apart, swearing that someday he would have that car. When he set his sights on something, he wasn't easily dissuaded . . . like the car, like a wife.

He decided he really didn't want to leave the city just yet and began walking again. The sights and sounds of Dallas never ceased to thrill and dismay him. The towering buildings, the cluttered streets, the narrow alleyways. People everywhere, coming and going, hurrying and strolling, climbing out of limousines or waiting impatiently at stoplights . . . surely somewhere in this great sprawling city there was a woman for him.

He knew where he had made his mistake, of course. He had been too blunt with the frosty-eyed, auburn-haired matchmaking woman. But things were much more straightforward in the wastelands of Alaska, and if Shane had been any good at gilding the lily, he could have no doubt found a bride in the conventional manner.

The trouble was, he didn't know anybody in Dallas except Jack. Jack had done his part in taking him around to the clubs, cotillions and by-invitation-only parties, but the women Shane met at those places fell into three categories: vacuous debutantes who wouldn't know a frying pan if it hit them in the face, hard-eyed executive women who spent an inordinate amount of time trying to prove how much smarter they were than he, and overly made-up party girls whose interest in him waned when the sun came up. Was it too much to ask for a nice, normal woman who wanted nothing more than to settle down and raise a family and let him love her?

Jack had assured him that if anybody could find that woman, Matchmakers could. Well, Jack had been wrong.

It irritated Shane when he thought of the contempt in Cassie Averil's green eyes as he'd outlined his needs for her. What would a woman like that know about men and women, anyway? He should have asked if *she* was married. You can't sell a product if you've never tried it.

But after a while the irritation turned to amusement as he replayed the conversation in his head. He supposed he had come off sounding like a caveman, but he couldn't help it; that was just his way. If she had given him a chance, he might have been able to make a better impression, but it didn't matter now. He was back to square one, and obviously he was going to have to think of something else.

Maybe, he thought only half facetiously, he *should* place an ad in the paper.

He walked down boulevards and side streets, pausing to look in the windows of jewelry stores and fancy dress shops, and before too long the sour memory of the unpleasant encounter was completely wiped away by his fascination with the city. He stopped in a pastry shop and bought something flaky and cream-filled, and by the time he wiped his fingers and tossed the napkin into a curbside trash can, all was right with the world. Sweets were such a rarity in the Great Northwest that now his taste for them was insatiable, and had he been a less active man he would have been fat within three months of stepping off the boat in Seattle.

He was no longer interested in any of the errands he had planned for the afternoon and started walking back toward the car, peering in shop windows and wondering if he dared call up Jack and hint for an invitation to supper. That would make three times this week. And though Jack's sister, who kept house for Jack and always had room for one more at her table, seemed to like him, Shane was afraid he was going to wear out his welcome if he wasn't careful.

Eventually he found himself in front of a pet store, and he grinned as he remembered Miss Averil's parting words. He tapped on the glass. A brown-and-white ball of fur with a bearded muzzle scurried over to the window and scratched on the pane. Shane grinned again and started to walk away. Then he stopped.

As far back as Shane could remember, he had wanted only three things out of life: a red Corvette, a big, comfortable home and a family. The first two were his, and as for the third . . . well, he supposed he had to start somewhere.

He went inside.

A few moments later Shane emerged with a brown-and-white puppy tucked under one arm and a sales slip in his pocket. On the sidewalk he held the puppy up and looked into its big brown eyes. "Well, Whiskers, you're not exactly what I had in mind when I went shopping this afternoon, but I guess you'll have to do. Three meals a day, a warm bed and all the squirrels you can chase. What more could anybody ask for?''

The puppy licked Shane's face and grinned happily. Shane grinned back. ''Maybe,'' he added as he started toward the car, ''at least *you'll* appreciate what I have to offer.''

Two

Cassie didn't come up with the solution to all her financial problems overnight, but she did come up with one important resolution: she wasn't going to let this business go without a fight. And she would never again be as rude to a client as she had been to Shane Bartlett.

Matchmaking was a family tradition that had begun with Cassie's grandmother back in the prewar years when Dallas was a boomtown and Ellen Craigston-Averil, newly arrived from Virginia and dripping of old money and social status, had made it her business to see that the raw, bustling oil town was made fit for civilized people. It began with a few letters: *Darling, my son is moving out your way with his new company. Do see that he meets some nice girl, will you?*

or *My dear friends the Longfords are passing through with their lovely daughter. I assured them they could count on you to see that the child met the right sort of companions.* It was all very quaint and old-fashioned and Grandma Averil had established a place for herself.

Cassie's mother had been the first to realize that what was done for love could also be done for money. Dallas in the postwar years was growing so fast and in such diverse directions that the old-fashioned methods of forming social relationships were simply not reliable anymore. She had established a "social club" long before anyone had thought of dating services, but the old-fashioned rules still applied. She screened backgrounds, made introductions, gave chaperoned dinner parties and, with her uncanny sense for compatibility, soon gained a reputation for making marriages that lasted.

By the time Cassie came along with her major in psychology and a lifetime of observing her mother and grandmother at work, the family business seemed a natural. And when Cassie's parents retired to Florida five years ago, Cassie was ready to bring the matchmaking business into the twentieth century.

She lay in bed with her eyes closed against the haze of morning sunlight, listening to the clock radio and trying to figure out where she had gone wrong. Certainly there was nothing wrong with her methods. She had kept the best of her mother's skills—hands-on service and attention to detail—and combined it with her own field of specialty to form a flawless method for bringing compatible couples together. She refused to rely on computers or random chance, as so many dating services did, and the extra effort paid off. Some of the relationships she arranged lasted as long as six months and the couples invariably parted friends— only to return to her for another "perfect match." Cassie wasn't bothered in the least by the fact that she rarely added a wedding picture to the collection on the walls formed by her mother and grandmother. Marriage was just another of those romantic trappings that had no place in the modern world, and she was glad for it. If everyone got married, no one would renew his contract with her and her profit margin would take a more desperate dive than it already had.

Undoubtably her only failing was poor management. With the new trend toward monogamy the business climate had looked better than ever, and she had plunged into the expensive downtown property and all the trappings without thought for the consequences. Following the family tradition, she spent an inordinate amount of time and effort on each client, concentrating on quality and not quantity. She was extravagant. She was a perfectionist. She wasn't, in short, a very good businesswoman.

She sighed and rolled over in bed, then grunted as a soft weight landed on her chest. She opened her eyes and squinted into the amber gaze of a gray-and-white cat. "Hello, you little tramp. Out all night again, huh? Still looking for the perfect romance?" She scratched the cat absently behind the ears. "Take it from an expert, kid. There's no such thing."

The cat nuzzled Cassie's face as though in protest, and Cassie sneezed. She was allergic to cats, but had never had the heart to tell Fluffy so. After the third sneeze, Cassie pushed the cat away and got out of bed, rubbing her itchy face and combing her hair back with her fingers. Fluffy jumped down from the bed with a disdainful twitch of her tail, and Cassie watched her in sleepy amusement. Life would be much easier if people were as uncomplicated as cats.

After a while she got up, put on her glasses and made her way to the closet. She grimaced at the full-length reflection of herself in the mirrored closet doors. Rumpled nightshirt, limp, shoulder-length hair, pale skin—she looked every one of her twenty-nine and a half years that morning. She leaned close to the mirror, lifted her glasses, put them back again and frowned over what were definitely the first signs of tiny crow's-feet on the outside corner of her left eye. "Great," she muttered. "That's what I get for devoting my life to the selfless service of others. Worry lines and overdue bills."

She slid open the closet doors and spent a moment staring at her uninspired wardrobe. She had three suits for the office: one black, one gray and one navy, all of which were worn with a choice of five white blouses, not one much distinguishable from the other. If there was one thing she hated about her work, it was being required to go to the office every day looking like a mortician, but she had learned early on the importance of dressing for success.

It was crucial that she obtain the confidence of her clients, because so much of the process revolved around the nuances that were revealed in a personal interview. People felt comfortable with Emma; her motherly, unpretentious manner put everyone at ease, which was one of her biggest assets. But with an attractively groomed, even stylish young woman, men tended to clam up and women felt threatened. No matter how she tried, Cassie couldn't make herself look motherly, so she opted for a neuter appearance instead. No one could feel defensive around a woman who was so undistinguished as to practically fade into the woodwork, and that was exactly the effect Cassie was aiming for.

But, God, she got tired of black and gray! And after noticing the crow's-feet, spending the day confined in one of those ugly costumes seemed like cruel and unusual punishment. On impulse she took out a green linen skirt and jacket with a paisley blouse. She held the outfit up before her and smiled approvingly into the mirror. The skirt was flared, the jacket was nipped at the waist, and the color magnified her eyes in a most flattering way. It was, in short, completely inappropriate for the office, and today Cassie didn't care. She needed self-esteem more than she needed self-image, and even if she wasn't much of a businesswoman today, she could at least look like a *woman*. Besides, who cared what she looked like in an empty office? And the way things had been going lately, the office would probably stay empty.

Perhaps there was something to color therapy, Cassie thought, because as she showered and dressed she actually began to feel more confident. There was, after all, no big mystery to success in business, any more than there was anything mystical about finding a compatible mate. All it took was planning, forethought and the right formula. And if there was anyone who could find that formula, it was Cassie Averil.

Shane was awakened at daybreak by the sound of hammers and saws. When the best architect in the city recommended the best contractor, that contractor made sure his crews were on the site before sunup and worked until dusk. Shane could have done with a little less enthusiasm and a little more peace and quiet, but he couldn't fault the progress of the construction.

He rubbed his face and swung his feet over the side of the bed, and barely missed stepping in a puddle. Whiskers sat nearby, looking at him expectantly. Shane returned the dog's gaze with a little less charity. "The lady was wrong," he muttered. "A dog is not the answer to all my problems."

The contractor had promised his house would be finished by the end of the month. Meanwhile, Shane was living in a one-room construction trailer which, all things considered, was more luxurious than the surroundings in which he had spent most of his life. The automatic coffee maker had already prepared its brew, so Shane pulled on a pair of jeans, poured a cup of coffee and took the dog and his breakfast outside.

No matter what was wrong with the world, the morning air and the morning view never failed to put it right again. The puppy scampered off to do the things puppies do, and Shane sat on the steps of the trailer, sipping his coffee and contentedly looking around at what was, as far as the eye could see, all his.

He had bought Long Acre, lock, stock and barrel, from a cattleman who was moving his operation to

Australia. The first thing he had done was sell off all the stock. The cattle were a picturesque touch, but they sounded like entirely too much work. The second thing he had done was bulldoze the perfectly good ranch house to the ground. No one seemed surprised; Texans were used to extravagant gestures. And the third thing he had done, even before he started construction on the house, was to build a swimming pool. The best hours of his life, so far, had been spent lying around that pool, doing absolutely nothing.

There were pecan groves and streams, rolling hills and flat, verdant meadows. A twenty-acre lake was stocked with bass and a field seeded for quail. There were even stables and some horses that experts told him were very fine stock, which he had decided to keep because he thought he might someday like to learn to ride. And in the midst of all this, less than two hundred yards from where he sat, rose his house—a sprawling two stories of rich red brick with terraces and patios, six bedrooms, seven baths, a wine cellar, an indoor pool and every modern amenity known to man. All in all, it was paradise.

And it meant nothing unless he had somebody to share it with.

He looked around when he heard the sound of a vehicle rounding the curve in the long driveway, and a gray Mercedes came into view. He lifted his hand in greeting as the car stopped and Jack Sanders got out. "That's what I like," he said as Jack approached. "A man who takes his job seriously."

Jack grinned and gestured toward the construction crew. "Everybody knows the architect doesn't show up on the job site unless something's got to be ripped out and rebuilt. So I like to come out every once in a while just to put the fear of God into those guys. Keeps them on their toes, and when I tell them everything is going along just fine, they're so grateful they work twice as hard." He pulled up a lawn chair and sat down. "So, you got anything you want ripped out or redesigned?"

Shane chuckled and shook his head. At that moment Whiskers came around the side of the trailer, sniffing the ground and wagging his tail. "How about a doghouse?"

"Well, look at that." Jack held out his hand, and the puppy came bounding over, circled Jack's chair a couple of times and scampered away again. "You're not wasting any time settling down to country living. What's he supposed to be?"

"I don't know. Some kind of Saint Bernard, I think."

"Forget the doghouse. I'd better start designing another wing. So." He settled back in his chair and regarded Shane with friendly, sun-narrowed eyes. "How'd it go with the matchmaker yesterday?"

"Do you want some coffee?"

"Does that mean it didn't go too well?"

Shane smothered a sheepish grin. "She kicked me out."

"Cassie Averil?" Jack's eyebrows shot up with astonishment. "Now that I can't believe. What'd you do, make a pass at her?"

"Of course not. I just did what I was supposed to do—told her what I wanted. She acted like she was a mother superior and I'd been caught climbing over the convent wall.''

Jack shifted his weight and nodded thoughtfully. He was a good-size man—testament to what a woman's cooking could do—and the lawn chair squeaked a little in protest. "I should have seen it coming."

Shane looked at him curiously. "What?"

Jack seemed to hesitate a minute, then came to a decision. He said, "I haven't known you very long, Shane, but I like you, and I think any woman would be damn lucky to have you. So what I'm going to tell you now, I'm telling you for your own good.

"You've been living in a man's world too long. You work hard, you fight your fights, you keep to the straight trail, and as long as you keep your eyes peeled for trouble, you get along okay. But here in civilization, as much as I hate to admit it, it's a woman's world, and things are a little more complicated. Women like finesse, you see. They like to take things slow. And a woman like Miss Cassie—well, she takes great pride in doing things right. You can't just walk up to her like you would a man and lay your cards on the table. There's got to be a little game playing first."

Shane frowned into his coffee. "Sounds like an awful lot of trouble to me."

"Exactly my point," Jack said immediately. "Finding the right woman *is* a lot of trouble. Some men go their whole life and never find her. You can't rush a thing like this, Shane. Look around, give it a lot of thought, take some time."

"I've thought about it," Shane responded forcefully. "I've spent thirty-two years thinking about it.

That's half a lifetime. The way I figure it, I don't have any time to waste. That was the whole idea behind this marriage broker business in the first place."

Jack shook his head sadly. "I swear I've never seen the like in my life. A good-looking fella like you, great big new house with two pools and a hot tub, not a care in the world. You should be out painting this town three different shades of red, son. That swimming pool should be crawling with willing young things every night of the week. They ought to be dripping off you like honey from a tree, and all you can think about is diaper bags and home cooking." He shook his head again. "Craziest thing I ever heard of."

Shane finished his coffee. "That's what I want, Jack. A man ought to know what he wants."

"I reckon so." Jack looked at him for another moment. "Your mind's made up, then?"

"Sure is."

Jack sighed. "Well, then, I think you'd better give Miss Cassie another chance. And go a little easy on her this time."

Shane winced and repressed a shudder. "Go back to Attila the Hun? I don't think so."

"You want results, don't you?"

"I'd rather wrestle a polar bear. At least then I'd have a sporting chance."

"There's always my sister."

Shane looked at him uncertainly. "Your sister is forty-five years old."

"But single."

"And—no offense, Jack—but some people might say she's just a little on the plump side."

Jack grinned. "A hell of a country cook."

Shane considered it for a moment, weighing his options. Then he got to his feet. "I think I'll give the matchmaker another shot," he said, but he wasn't happy about it. Not one bit.

Cassie strode into the office, announcing energetically, "Okay, this is what we're going to do. Write a check for the furniture and send it to the telephone company. Write a check to the telephone company and send it to the furniture people. That'll buy us some time while they get it straightened out. Meanwhile, call Frank Lender and see if he's free tonight. Then get Elizabeth Michaels on the phone."

"Perfect," exclaimed Emma. She was already dialing. "I don't know why I didn't think of Frank before. He's perfect for her." Her eyes twinkled as she covered the mouthpiece with her hand. "Glad to see you're back to your old form."

Cassie made a circle of her thumb and forefinger and sailed into her office.

Twenty minutes later she had made reservations for a quiet booth at an intimate restaurant that both Elizabeth and Frank favored, she had advised Elizabeth on what to wear and had ordered roses in Frank's name. A little atmosphere never hurt; it was all part of the game. She had briefed both parties on the personal history of the other, and it looked like a promising evening. She didn't even allow herself a moment for self-congratulations, but immediately pulled out another file.

Cassie supposed she was a voyeur in a way, deriving vicarious satisfaction from delving into other people's psyches, discovering things about them that they themselves didn't even know, and then finding, through skill and hard work, another person whose needs and sensitivities meshed with the first. But the satisfaction Cassie felt in her work was due less to the reward of a job well done than to the process itself: simple, predictable, reliable. Introvert plus extrovert equals stimulation. Like to like equals happiness. Need plus fulfillment equals love. The intricate process of analysis, comparison and rejection was absorbing and challenging, and Cassie quickly became lost in her work.

At midmorning there was a tap on her door, and Cassie looked up from her charts and graphs to see Shane Bartlett standing there. "I got a dog," he said. "It wasn't the same."

Her pulse actually skipped a beat, and she wasn't certain whether it was from surprise, remembered embarrassment for her behavior yesterday or simply from the fact that in a city that was known for its rugged, good-looking men, Shane Bartlett could have easily posed for a Chamber of Commerce welcome poster.

He was dressed much as he had been yesterday—in jeans that hugged his hips and thighs, an open leather vest and a dark belt with a big silver buckle. His shirt was white, with the sleeves turned up to the elbows, and it looked magnificent against his deep tan. And today the boots showed signs of polishing, which didn't help their appearance much, but did at least show he was willing to try.

He stood with one foot over the threshold and the door only partially open, as though unsure of his welcome. Cassie stood quickly and smiled. "Mr. Bartlett, how nice to see you again. Please come in."

Shane hesitated. All the way into town he had been having second thoughts, and he still wasn't sure what he was doing here. But in her green dress and multicolored blouse she looked less formidable than she had yesterday. She looked, in fact, almost feminine. And her smile of welcome, if it wasn't genuine, was certainly a very good imitation. Cautiously he came inside, but kept his hand on the doorknob.

"Jack said I ought to give you another chance," he said. Then, realizing that might sound a little ungracious, and not wanting to set her off again, he added quickly, "I guess I might have come on too strong yesterday."

With all of her newfound resolutions for success in mind, Cassie was forced to admit, "Perhaps we both did."

Shane almost relaxed. This wasn't as hard as he had expected. "So, how about starting over?"

For the space of five seconds Cassie argued with herself. She needed the money. She needed Jack Sanders's goodwill. But she didn't have a prayer in heaven of finding Shane Bartlett a wife, or even a date, and her respect for women everywhere rebelled at the thought of even trying. On the other hand, how could she know unless she tried? And Emma was right: this would be the ultimate test of her skills as an analyst and the final proof of her theories of compatibility. Shane Bartlett didn't want just a date; he wanted a wife. How could she turn down such an opportunity? Surely there was a woman for every man, and if she didn't believe that, she shouldn't be in the business.

In the end, she succumbed to the sense of challenge—or perhaps it was simple greed—and she smiled at him. "Why don't you come in and have a seat? Close the door."

He still looked hesitant, but he did as she asked.

To cover her uneasiness over the growing conviction that this was a mistake, Cassie began to speak hurriedly. "Let me tell you a bit about the way we operate. My clients generally sign a contract that entitles them to use my service for a year. The initial fee covers the cost of setup and file maintenance and is renewable at a substantial discount. Of course, you understand I can't make any guarantees, but what I try to do when someone comes in here is to gather an extensive psychological profile on him or her, and make introductions based on what I know about the client's personality, temperament, values, goals, all that sort of thing. As I may have said before, we don't operate in the manner of a traditional dating service in that we leave nothing to chance. You shouldn't expect to have to meet more than two or three women before you find someone with whom it's possible to form a firm relationship. That, after all, is the advantage of employing a service like this—it eliminates the hassle and rejection of the singles scene. You can be assured that when I do introduce you to someone, I've done my very best to eliminate the guesswork."

She couldn't tell, from his expression, whether he was impressed or whether he had, in fact, understood anything she had said. Cassie took a breath and gave him a smile that was far more confident than she felt. "So, I guess the first thing we should discuss is the fee."

She took a slip of paper and felt a momentary twinge of guilt when she wrote down a figure that was twice her normal fee. She passed it across the desk to him.

Shane examined it for a moment without any visible reaction. Then he said, "I'll tell you what. You find me a wife by the end of the month and you can add an extra zero to that number. My house is going to be finished by then," he explained, and pushed the paper back to her. "I'd like to have a bride ready to move in."

Cassie stared at him and thought, *This man can't be for real. He simply can't be.* She had thought that yesterday must have been a fluke, a mistake or misunderstanding on both their parts, yet here he was today making even more outrageous demands. A month. Placing an order for a wife as if he were ordering a new carpet or drapes to complete his house.

And finally it sank in. *An extra zero.* Ten times the amount she had written down which was already twice as much as she usually charged.... An extra zero! She could pay her rent, she could *buy* office furniture instead of leasing it, she could install a computer system for bookkeeping, she could pay Emma's back salary, not to mention her own, she could stay in operation for the rest of the year without lifting a finger. Her business, in short, would be saved.

Cassie cleared her throat. She looked at the slip of paper again. She looked back at him. "You are serious, aren't you?"

Shane was getting a little tired of hearing that question, but he tried not to let it show. If it was this much trouble just hiring a matchmaker, what did he have to look forward to when the actual selection process began? He answered as patiently as he could. "Yes, ma'am, I'm serious."

Cassie returned her gaze to the paper, mentally inserting another zero. *You can't do this, Cassie. It's not right. It's not ethical, it's not moral, it may not even be legal.*

But another zero...

Her voice sounded a little hoarse as she said, "Mr. Bartlett, did you ever hear the expression, 'money can't buy love'?"

"I'm not trying to buy love," he explained, shifting restlessly. "I'm buying your services." He smiled. "Love just comes naturally."

She would be a fool to accept his offer. She couldn't possibly find someone to fit his specifications even if she had wanted to. And she didn't want to, even if she had a year instead of less than a month.

Carefully she said, "I would need half the fee up front as a deposit."

He took out his checkbook.

She would find someone for him, Cassie vowed fervently, if she had to go through the entire Dallas-Fort Worth phone book and start knocking on doors.

But then he gave the check and an attack of conscience seized her. This wasn't a joke. She had more money in her hand right now than she had seen in the past three months combined, and she had a horrible feeling she was getting in over her head. She thought of all those pictures of happily married couples on the walls that had lured him in. Was that fraud?

Hating herself even as she spoke, she said, "Mr. Bartlett, I've got to be honest with you. We arrange dates, not marriages. And," she continued, suffering an almost physical pain as the admission was torn from her, "sometimes those dates aren't one hundred percent successful. You can't expect any guarantees."

He looked mildly surprised. "Ma'am, when I buy a car I expect the engine to run. When I build a house I expect the plumbing to work. You just gave me your word and I just gave you my money. Now, can you find me a wife or not?"

Cassie, Cassie, don't be a fool....

She had devoted her life to developing a process by which the element of chance could be taken out of interpersonal relationships. For years she had told herself that the only reason her theory wasn't one hundred percent successful was because the people involved weren't sufficiently motivated. No one wanted to expend any effort or make a commitment to success. She couldn't work with flawed material.

Well, here was a man who was motivated. He was making a commitment. He was putting himself in her hands. Shane Bartlett was the perfect candidate to prove the validity of her methods.

He was also stubborn, opinionated, demanding and filled with preconceived notions—and all that was obvious from a mere five-minute acquaintance with him. Who knew what other undesirable traits were lurking just beneath the surface? She had no idea what she was getting into.

But then again, neither did he. And the bottom line was, did she believe in herself or not?

Her hand tightened on the check. She lifted her eyes to his. "Yes, Mr. Bartlett," she said firmly, "I can find you a wife. But you're going to have to cooperate. You're going to have to give up some of your unrealistic expectations and put yourself completely in my hands."

Shane blinked, a little taken aback. "What do you mean, unrealistic expectations?"

Cassie leaned forward earnestly. "You've got to trust me completely. From this moment on I'm going to be your shadow. I'm going to know you better than your own mother does. You're going to tell me things you wouldn't tell your priest and you're going to listen to me when I tell you what to do. As of this very minute, you're turning yourself completely over to me. Is that understood? One hundred percent cooperation. That's the only way this thing can work. So, if you have any doubts, you'd better tell me now."

There was a fervor in her eyes that overwhelmed Shane, and he wasn't sure he liked her reference to "work"—any more than he liked the idea of being told what to do by a woman, especially when it came to something as touchy as romance. But then again he had to give her some credit for knowing what she was doing, and there were surely worse things than putting himself completely in the hands of a woman who looked as pretty as she did in that green dress.

He shrugged. "No. No doubts."

"Good." She placed her hands palm down on the desk and braced her shoulders. "Then we have a deal?"

"Fine." Cassie tried to temper her enthusiasm with professionalism as she reached into her desk and took out a stack of papers. She inserted the papers into a folder and passed them across the desk to him. "Then the first thing you need to do is fill out this personality profile."

Shane managed not to groan out loud. "There must be two hundred questions here," he complained as he flipped through the pages.

"Two hundred and fifty. Better get started."

Shane gave her a rebellious look, but Cassie stared him down. At last he took up a pen and began filling in the blanks.

The first few questions were easy. Age, sex, name. When he got to the part about religion, he looked up. "I was raised in a Methodist's Children's Home. Does that count?"

"You were an orphan, then?" Cassie thought that could explain a lot.

"Yeah." He frowned impatiently. "Listen, what I don't understand is why you have to have all this information about *me*. I'm the one who's doing the looking. Why can't you just line up some women and let me ask the questions?"

Several retorts sprang to mind, and Cassie squelched them. She replied patiently, "I thought I had explained all that, Mr. Bartlett." She could see another objection forming, so she added, "I have to have the same information on all my clients. After all, I have to make sure I'm not setting someone up with the Son of Sam, don't I?"

"We have a deal."

"Well..." He seemed only slightly mollified as he flipped through the pages again. "That makes sense, I guess. But this could take the rest of the day."

"At the rate you're going it could."

With a sigh he picked up the pen again. Cassie, meanwhile, took the opportunity to make a few notes of her own.

On the surface, his strongest asset was his physical appearance. He had a lean, athletic build, strong thighs, good hands. Probably a strong libido. If matching people were as simple as breeding horses, she would have no problem at all. He was left-handed, which surprised her. Many creative people were left-handed, and Shane Bartlett didn't seem the creative type at all.

After a moment she inquired curiously, "How long were you in the children's home?"

"Off and on, about twelve years. My parents were killed on the highway when I was two, and I didn't have any other relatives."

"That must have been a hard way to grow up."

"Not really." He continued to fill in blanks as he spoke. "I mean, you hear a lot of garbage about foster homes and such, but I never had any problems—except for moving from one place to another and getting used to new families. I didn't much care for that."

Aha, thought Cassie's psychoanalytical mind. "Were you ever adopted?"

"No, and I never could understand that. I was cute as the dickens."

Cassie tried to hide a grin with the corner of her hand, but Shane saw it and his eyes crinkled. *Nice smile,* she observed. *Warm eyes.*

And he surprised her by observing, "You know, you're not half bad when you smile. I'll bet people would be a lot friendlier to you if you did it more often."

Immediately Cassie erased the smile and turned back to her notes. *Outspoken,* she wrote. *Very straightforward.* "I'm sure you meant that as a compliment, Mr. Bartlett, but for now let's just concentrate on you, shall we?"

Abruptly he closed the folder. "How would you like to go get some ice cream?"

She looked up at him, startled. "What?"

"There's a place just down the street with benches in the sun. I've got to tell you, I've been inside for almost half an hour and the walls are starting to close in."

"But it's only ten-thirty in the morning."

"Good." He got to his feet. "It won't spoil your lunch."

Cassie hesitated. Maybe, in his case, a hands-on interview would be more revealing, and he could always finish the profile at home. "All right," she conceded. "Maybe we could take a break for a little while. But you still have to fill out the form."

He folded the pages and tucked them into his pocket. "Later," he promised and opened the door.

On the way out, Cassie stopped by Emma's desk and gave her the check. "Put this in the bank *immediately*," she whispered.

Emma glanced at the check and her eyes widened. The older woman looked back at Cassie, but Cassie silenced her with a look. Turning back to Shane, she smiled pleasantly. "Shall we go?"

Three

It was a bright morning in early June, the streets smelled of gasoline fumes and asphalt and the sky was the famed Texas blue that could be found nowhere else on earth. Cassie loved Dallas, with its combination of new world enterprise and old world manners, its pioneer spirit and brazen pride, its international glamour and small-town friendliness. She loved the smell of the streets and the sound of traffic, the brash new buildings and quaint, intimate gathering places. She loved the way people moved, with purpose but leisure, as though they knew where they were going but were equally confident the world would wait for them to get there. Glancing at the man walking next to her, she decided Shane Bartlett fitted in perfectly here.

"So," she asked as they rounded a corner, "what made you decide to come to Dallas?"

"Well, to tell you the truth, there really wasn't much choice in my mind. You see, there aren't many local television stations in the places I worked, and even when there were, reception was kind of a hit-or-miss proposition. But no matter where I was somebody always managed to get a tape of *Dallas* through; it was about the only entertainment there was on a Saturday night. Everybody would gather at the local bar and watch it, or sometimes, if we were too far out for electricity, we made damn sure there was somebody with a battery-powered VCR. And let me tell you, if the chopper was late with mail and supplies, the men would gripe about missing green vegetables, but they'd get downright violent if they had to miss an episode of *Dallas*."

Cassie couldn't help grinning at the thought of a bunch of roughneck miners and pipeline workers huddled around a television set, addicted to a soap opera. "So you came here expecting fast deals and beautiful women in designer gowns?" All blond, of course, she added to herself.

"Nope." He took her elbow as they crossed the street, which Cassie thought was a nice gesture—old-fashioned and protective. He dropped her arm immediately when they reached the other side. "I came because it looked so warm. Everybody lounging by the pool, having breakfast on the terrace, drinking fancy drinks in frosted glasses. That's what I wanted—someplace warm."

Cassie shook her head a little, amused. "But it's not warm all the time, you know. It's not unusual to see twenty degrees here in the winter."

"Twenty degrees?" His tone was lightly scoffing. "Honey, that's not even nippy. I don't bother to get out my winter coat until it hits forty below."

She laughed and stepped inside the ice-cream parlor as he opened the door. Almost despite herself, she was beginning to like him.

Shane ordered a double strawberry and rocky road cone, and Cassie, though she really wasn't in the mood for ice cream at that hour, ordered a small cup of vanilla. "I knew you were a vanilla person," Shane commented, scooping up a handful of napkins on their way out. "Do you want to sit over there?"

He indicated a courtyard scattered with white iron benches and umbrellaed tables, and she nodded. "What does that mean, a vanilla person?"

"Nothing. Just that you're not very adventurous."

She shrugged. "Ice cream is ice cream."

He looked as though he wanted to respond to that, but decided it was more prudent not to.

Cassie chose a table in the shade of an umbrella, and Shane sat across from her, moving his chair into the sun. He leaned back, pushed his hat away from his face and tilted his face contentedly toward the sun. He reminded Cassie of a sleek, bronzed feline, basking in the desert warmth.

Cassie had to remind herself that there was no time to waste, that she wasn't here to admire Shane Bartlett's form. "Let's start with something simple," she said. "What do you like to do for recreation?"

"Eat ice cream."

"Besides that."

His eyes were half closed against the glare of the sun, his face turned at a slight angle away from her, and he enjoyed the ice-cream cone with an aggressive sensuality that Cassie found more captivating than she liked to admit. He scraped his teeth across the top of the mound, then ran his tongue across its breadth. He let the sweetness dissolve in his mouth, then tasted it from another angle, slowly, thoroughly, and with absorbed pleasure. She had never know a man who could give himself over so completely to so simple an experience. It was fascinating to watch.

"Mostly," he answered at leisure, "I like to lie in the sun and do nothing. By the pool."

His tongue circled the ice-cream cone with luxurious delight, making spirals and patterns with long, caressing strokes. Cassie became aware that her own ice cream was beginning to melt, and she picked up her spoon. "No," she said a little impatiently, "I mean, what do you like to *do*? Surely you must have some interests, hobbies, even an avocation."

He spared a moment away from his worship of the sun to slant a glance at her. "Avocation? Is that like work?"

"Sort of. It could be."

He turned his face back to the light and bit off the tip of an ice-cream spiral. His drawl was slow and lazy. "I've been working since I was twelve years old. Hard work, with sweat and blisters. Twenty years of that was enough for me, and I plan to spend the next twenty sitting in the sun and doing nothing. I don't ever want to hear the word *work* again. Or avocation, either.''

"Look, Mr. Bartlett, you've got to help me out here." Cassie tried to keep the frustration out of her voice. "We don't have a lot of time, and I'm trying to find out—"

"Fishing," he interrupted easily, taking another long swipe at the ice cream with his tongue. "I like to fish. And hunt."

Cassie released a pent-up breath. "Fine. Good. You like outdoor sports. Water skiing? Baseball? Boating?''

"Nope. Just fishing and hunting.''

"Is that what you like to do on a date? I'm trying to find out what you enjoy doing with a *woman*.''

He didn't look at her, but the slow, sensual curve of his lips was explicit. "Oh, the usual things.''

But Cassie was in no mood for games. Despite the shade of the umbrella, she was warm, though it might have had more to do with watching Shane soak up heat with the same greedy sensuality with which he caressed the ice-cream cone than the temperature of the day. She slipped off her jacket and hung it on the back of the chair. "Mr. Bartlett," she demanded carefully, "have you *ever* been out with a woman?''

"Of course I have.''

"All right, then, what did you do?''

He flattened the top of the cone with his teeth. "Well, generally, we'd meet at Sophie's—that's a bar— for a beer, then go back to her place. Or, if I happened to be in a city, we'd take in a movie and then go back to her place.''

"And?"

"And what?"

"And what then?" Cassie dug her spoon into the half-liquid ice cream and took perverse pleasure in goading him. "I mean, that's a pretty short evening. Not much time for developing social skills. You have a drink, you go back to her place, and . . . talk? Play pinochle? Knit sweaters? What?"

He slid his gaze toward her, eyes that were sun-gilded and heavily lidded, and murmured, "Lady, if you don't know what happened then, I'm definitely going to have to find myself a new matchmaker." He turned his attention back to his ice cream. "Kept warm," he said. "We kept warm."

Cassie arranged her spoon across the rim of the cup and dabbed her lips with a corner of the paper napkin. "I'm afraid, Mr. Bartlett, that the young women of Dallas will expect a somewhat more sophisticated form of entertainment than that."

He smiled, secretly and with infuriating confidence, to himself, but said nothing. Cassie, watching him devote himself to the ice-cream cone again with decadent abandon, had no difficulty picturing images to go along with that smile. Raw, animal sexuality, she observed with what she thought was admirable detachment. An unmitigated sensualist in every way. He must have had a lot of practice "keeping warm," and if all he had wanted was a date, this would have been the easiest assignment she had ever had.

He noticed her staring at him, and a glint of amusement came into his eyes. He held out the ice-cream cone. "Want a bite?"

For some reason, and to her great annoyance, Cassie blushed. "No thanks," she said curtly, and busily wadded up her napkin and stuffed it into her cup of melted ice cream. "We have quite a bit of ground to cover, and I'd appreciate it if you'd try to be a bit more cooperative."

Shane finished his ice-cream cone in three deliberate bites, then wiped his fingers on the napkin. For a time the so-called interview had been entertaining, even amusing, but he had a feeling Cassie Averil didn't think so. He didn't think he had ever met a more uptight woman, and he wondered if that was a result of city life, or just a normal part of her personality.

"Look," he said, "if you ask me, you're making this a lot harder than it has to be. I've told you before, all I want you to do is let me tell you what I want, and you supply the woman to fit the bill."

Cassie felt her shoulder muscles tighten with frustration. How many times did she have to explain this to him? "Mr. Bartlett," she said with exaggerated patience, "if it were that easy, you wouldn't have come to me. You could have found what you were looking for by yourself."

"If I had twenty or thirty years," he agreed, "and if I wanted to spend them squiring around one woman after the other only to find out she's not the one, after all. The thing is..." And for the first time he was uncomfortable, perhaps because for the first time he was forced to tell her something personal about himself. Perhaps it would have been easier to fill out the form, after all. "I'm not very good at that sort of thing. Playing games, impressing people. And I don't like it."

Cassie nodded thoughtfully, unsurprised. "You've spent most of your life alone."

"All of it," he corrected simply.

There was a moment of brief vulnerability in his gaze, then he looked away. And in that moment, brief though it was, Cassie experienced a twinge of empathy she had never expected to feel for him. Suddenly he was more than a challenge, more than the fee that would save her business, more, even, than the enormous gamble he represented. In that moment she was determined to succeed—not just for herself, but for him.

Making a concerted effort to keep her tone detached, she said, "Obviously, you're not happy being alone. Do you have any idea why you've been unable to find a woman you were willing to commit to before now?"

His eyes glinted with low-key amusement. "Because the ratio of men to women in Alaska is approximately sixteen to one?" he suggested.

Cassie's brows knit slightly in annoyance. She hadn't expected an answer that simple. "Because," she said, hoping to override his logic with her conviction, "you don't really know what you want as well as you think you do."

He laced his fingers together and stretched out his arms before him, seeming unimpressed. Cassie watched his shoulders tighten against the pliant leather of his vest, and the muscles of his upper arms flex and lengthen beneath his shirt. Nice form, she observed again. Very nice.

"How would you know?" he inquired without much real interest. "You won't even listen to me when I try to tell you what I want."

"Because," Cassie informed him, "that's my job. Between the profile form and this interview, I'll know things you would never think of telling me, and those are the keys to making a match—the things that even you aren't aware of."

Shane looked at her suspiciously, not liking the sound of that. "What if I don't fill out the form?"

Cassie hesitated. "That would make it more difficult, of course, but in the long run it doesn't matter. Within a week I'll know you better than you know yourself." The blatantly skeptical look in his eyes pushed her to add, "As a matter of fact, by the end of the day I'll be able to tell you things about yourself even you won't believe."

"What are you, some kind of mind reader or something?"

She smiled. "No. Just good at my job."

He seemed to consider that for a moment, then dismissed it with a shrug. "In the first place, I don't believe you. In the second place, it doesn't matter. You don't need to know about me. You need to know about *her*."

Rarely did Cassie come across a man who was so protective of his privacy, and that could only make her job more difficult. Obviously her current approach wasn't going to work, so she threw up her hands in a small gesture of resignation. "All right," she invited. "Let's talk about her."

"Great." Shane got to his feet, his expression pleased. "Do you mind if we walk while we talk? This place is starting to get a little crowded."

Two other couples had come out while they were sitting, and though Cassie would hardly call that a crowd, she thought it might be considered one to a man who had spent most of his life in the vast open spaces of Alaska. She picked up her jacket and her purse and let him lead the way.

He didn't turn back toward the office, but continued down the street at an easy pace, his fingers tucked into his front pockets and his head tipped back to catch the slant of the sun. It was already warm, and Cassie carried her jacket over her arm. She hoped he didn't intend to walk far.

"All right," she said, "let's look at your specifications one by one." From what she had been able to determine about him so far, he seemed like a fairly intelligent man, and even reasonable to some extent. She hoped to appeal to his better judgment by simply letting him hear his fantasies brought into the light of day. "First, if I recall, you said you didn't want your wife to work. Have you really thought about that?"

"Oh, I know all about women's lib and how everybody has a job these days," he answered, and Cassie was cautiously encouraged. At least he *had* heard of the role of the modern woman. "But," he continued, "I'm retired. I've got nothing tying me down. My time's my own, to travel, give a party if I want to, do things without planning for them. And I want my wife to be able to come along. She couldn't do that if she had a job. Make sense?"

Unfortunately it did. Cassie had to remind herself, as she conceded the point to him, that this wasn't a game of one-upmanship.

"And, of course," he continued easily, "I think the kids should have a full-time mother. I'm not interested in any woman who can't make up her mind between her family and her work."

Cassie seized on that. "A woman can do both, Mr. Bartlett. In fact, most people agree that a woman who is content in her work outside the home makes a more interesting, fulfilling companion. Do you really want to live with someone who never reads a newspaper or a book and who has absolutely nothing to say to you outside of the latest cute thing Junior did today?"

"I never said she couldn't read a newspaper," Shane replied, unconcerned. "And since I'm going to be home to see all the cute things Junior did, we'll have lots to talk about."

"You cannot keep a woman as a slave," Cassie said, perhaps a bit too forcefully. "You've got to consider the other person's happiness, or I promise you the relationship is doomed from the start. You've got to allow for—"

Shane stopped on the sidewalk and looked at her. His mild brown eyes were filled with patience and unshakable conviction. "Look," he said simply, "all I want is to settle down with one person for the rest of my life and raise a family. And if you're trying to tell me that there's not one woman in this city who wants the same thing, then it seems to me God just wasted his time inventing two sexes. I mean, that's what it's all about, isn't it? Going forth and multiplying?"

Cassie had absolutely no answer to that, and the fact frustrated her no end. "All right. We'll leave that for a minute." She started walking again. "The point I'm trying to make, Mr. Bartlett—"

"Could you call me Shane? Every time you say my name you make me feel like I should take my hat off and scoot down in my desk."

"Well, all right." She tried out his name a little awkwardly. "Shane..."

"Do you have a name?"

There she hesitated. "I've found that it's best, for professional relations—"

"Remember when you told me you were going to be my best friend? I don't usually call my best friends by their last names. Besides, I can never remember whether it's supposed to be Miss or Mrs. or Ms."

Cassie couldn't understand why he professed such discomfort in social situations; the easy warmth of his smile could easily melt the coldest female heart. After a moment she found herself returning that smile. "You could always call me, 'Hey You.'"

His smile turned into a grin, and Cassie reminded herself sternly that this was an interview, not a flirtation—and she was a little annoyed with herself for having forgotten, even for an instant. "My name is Cassandra—Cassie," she said. "You may call me whatever you feel comfortable with."

"Now that opens up some interesting possibilities," he murmured.

Cassie didn't glance at him. To have done so would have given him an opportunity to change the subject again. "As I was saying," she began determinedly.

"You were about to make another speech."

"I was about to say," she corrected, "that you simply can't be so rigid in your demands, and if you spend some time thinking about it, you'll see that I'm right."

"I've spent fifteen years thinking about it."

"You've spent fifteen years *fantasizing*," Cassie pointed out. "Daydreaming about all the things you didn't have and wished you did. And like most men, the things you've come up with are not only unrealistic, they offer very short-term satisfaction. For example, what if you met a woman who was perfect in every way, but couldn't cook?"

"Food's important to me," he argued. "I can't cook, so it only makes sense that my wife should."

"Nonsense. Hire a housekeeper. Or learn to cook yourself."

"It wouldn't be the same. A woman who doesn't like to cook generally doesn't like to eat. I want someone who enjoys the same things I do."

"*You* like to eat, but you don't know how to cook."

"It's not the same for a man."

It was all Cassie could do to keep from slapping the palm of her hand against her head in frustration. "All right," she said, drawing a breath through her teeth. "What about this business of 'talking too much'? Surely you don't intend to spend the rest of your life with a sullen, simpering female who can't even carry on a conversation?"

"I'm not a real talkative person myself," he replied implacably. He cast a sideways glance at her and added, "Generally. I need a woman who understands I like my peace and quiet sometimes."

Cassie was within a hairbreadth of being convinced that he *did* know more about what he wanted than she did. But she was too stubborn to admit it. "I suppose there's no point in trying to convince you that the perfect woman doesn't always wear a size eight and have blond hair and blue eyes."

"You can't argue with a man's taste."

No, that she couldn't do.

They had walked several blocks, and Cassie's feet were beginning to burn. She could feel her blouse sticking to her back in several places, and her hair was beginning to frizz around her face with perspiration. But she wasn't ready to give up yet. "Have you ever known a woman like the one you just described?"

He seemed to review the candidates in his head. "Not really. One or two came close."

"All right, the one that came closest—why didn't you marry her?"

"Oh, I don't know. Lots of reasons. I guess mostly because something didn't click."

"Or could it be because once you got to know her, you found out she wasn't really what you wanted at all?"

"Well, sure, I guess that was it. No spark."

"So you see, your criteria didn't really work as well as you thought," she pointed out smugly. "And that's why I'm going to use different criteria."

"Like what?"

"Like finding out what you need, not what you want."

"There's a difference?"

"Always."

After a moment he shrugged. "Okay, I'm game. What do I need?"

She paused on the street and looked him over speculatively. "I don't think I'm ready to tell you that yet."

Shane was beginning to feel the smallest edge of frustration. This was turning out to be far more complicated than he had expected, and he had an unpleasant suspicion he was wasting his time...not to mention his money.

"Look," he said, "I don't want to hurt your feelings, but I've got to be honest with you. You've been talking to me all morning, and I not only didn't understand half of what you said, but I don't think you do, either. Are you trying to tell me that if you fix me up with someone I *don't* want I'll be happy?"

Cassie smiled and shook her head. "Not exactly."

"Then you've got some kind of secret formula for romance that's supposed to make me fall in love with whatever woman you pull out of your hat?"

"There's a formula, yes," she agreed. "But it has nothing to do with romance. And as for love—well, that's a highly misunderstood term."

Shane's skepticism grew. He was sure he wasn't going to like the answer she gave to his next question. "What do you mean by that?"

"I mean," she answered easily, "people have built a whole mystique out of something that doesn't really exist—not in the accepted sense, anyway. Love is nothing more than need—on a sexual, mental and emotional level. When two people stimulate that need in each other, even if the need is only partially fulfilled, you have love. Or, as I like to call it, success.

Compatibility is only one ingredient in that success, which is why it really isn't important for me to know what you think you want. It takes an objective observer who knows *both* the people involved to put all the ingredients together successfully."

Shane was feeling more and more uneasy about this whole arrangement. First, she told him he didn't know his own mind. Then she told him it didn't matter what he wanted. Now she was telling him there was no such thing as love. What kind of matchmaker was she, anyway?

He took off his hat and squinted at the sun, running his fingers uncertainly through his curls. "Look, maybe I should think about this some more...."

She ignored him and scanned the street opposite them. Suddenly she touched his arm. "Let's cross here."

"What for?" But when she led him toward the door of an exclusive men's shop, he knew what for, and he balked. "Now what do you think you're doing?"

"We're buying you some new clothes."

"I've got all the clothes I need."

She looked him over once with an expression that left little doubt about her opinion of his taste. "You've been out of the social scene for a long time," she explained, "and Dallas can be a pretty demanding town. You're going to look your best before you go out with anyone on my list."

She started to open the door, but he put his hand above hers, holding it closed. "Now let's just get one thing straight," he said firmly. "I am who I am and

I'm not changing for anybody. If you think you're going to make me over with a new suit of clothes—"

"Don't be silly," Cassie responded impatiently. "Nobody's trying to change you. All I'm talking about is making a good impression. Don't you think your date is going to go to a little extra trouble fixing her hair and putting on makeup and picking out a dress? There's no reason in the world why you shouldn't give her the same courtesy."

Cassie could see him trying to think of arguments, but after a moment the stubborn expression on his face faded to mild disgruntlement. "You're the bossiest woman I ever did meet," he muttered, and removed his hand from the door.

Twenty minutes later Shane stepped out of the dressing room in a nicely cut summer-weight suit with western shoulders and trim pants. Cassie was pleased with her instincts and impressed with the transformation. The oyster shell color enhanced his bronze shading without making him look monochromatic, and the casual style suited his lanky build perfectly. He would make heads turn in any restaurant or club in the city, though she suspected he could have done that without the help of a new suit.

"Well, what do you think?" she asked.

Shane bent his arms at the elbows, then held them straight out, checking the length of the cuffs. He turned to the mirror, smoothed down the jacket and peered at himself sideways. "Not bad," he admitted. "Better than I thought it would be. I can live with this."

"Of course you can. I told you, I know what I'm doing."

"Perhaps an inch longer in the cuffs," the clerk commented.

"Right," agreed Cassie. "And maybe a little tighter through here." She made a small tuck in one leg of the pants with her fingers. Shane seemed startled at her touch, but he didn't protest. "And the waist..."

She pinched his waistband with her fingers and felt the heat and firmness of his abdomen beneath the material of his shirt. He stepped back, as though her touch were an electric thing, and she, just as quickly, jerked her hand away, embarrassed. Until that moment the interchange had been impersonal, and Cassie, in fact, had hardly been aware of what she was doing. Now she was acutely aware of how close she was standing, half bent over to examine the fit of the suit with his pelvis and long legs filling up her vision, and she imagined she could still feel the warmth of his body on her fingertips.

She cleared her throat and moved away quickly. "Well," she said to the clerk, "you make whatever alterations you think are necessary. And let's have two more in the materials we looked at."

She had a selection of ties over her arm and picked one at random, holding it close to Shane's face. There was no way she could avoid looking at him then, and she was prepared for the knowing, almost intimate glint of speculation in his eyes. She stared him down coolly. "Don't wear blue." She discarded the tie. "This topaz is more your color...." She held it up to make sure. "Or this green."

"I don't wear ties," Shane pointed out.

"Mr. Sedgton, where is that pink shirt I was looking at?"

Shane took an adamant step back, both hands raised in protest. "And I don't wear pink!"

"Don't be silly. Lots of men wear pink." She took the folded shirt Mr. Sedgton provided and held it beneath Shane's neck. "Besides, it's not really pink. It's more of a peach. And it looks nice. Let's try the yellow."

Shane endured her ministrations for another three shirts and five ties with long-suffering silence, but Cassie could see rebellion building in his eyes. When she took a step back and looked critically down at his boots, he said forcefully, "No, ma'am. I don't get rid of these boots for anybody. You can dress me up in your fancy suit and put me in a tie and maybe, just maybe, you can get me to wear pink, but you're not taking these boots."

Cassie could see she had already pushed her luck as far as it would go, so she shrugged and turned back to Mr. Sedgton. "How soon can you have these things delivered?"

"We can have one suit ready this afternoon, but the others may take until late tomorrow."

"That's fine," approved Cassie, "but make certain you have one suit finished today. Mr. Bartlett has a date tonight."

Shane, who was shrugging out of the jacket on his way to the dressing room, stopped. The surprise in his expression showed that he was busily reworking his opinion of Cassie's skills as a matchmaker. "Already? You've got someone already?"

"Yes," Cassie replied. "Me." She couldn't tell whether the expression on his face was astonishment or dismay, and she wasn't sure she really wanted to know. Without giving a misunderstanding any time to develop, she added, "Think of it as a practice run."

"Practice!" There was no mistaking his expression now. It was sheer astonishment, liberally mixed with outrage as he stared at her. "You expect me to *audition* for a date?"

Cassie waved a dismissing hand. "Not at all. It's just that I need to see how you conduct yourself on a date, what your tastes in entertainment are, what you expect from the evening...and what you contribute, to be honest. Talking to you is one thing, but I really need to see how you behave in public."

"Like whether I eat with my fingers or spit on the table?"

Cassie realized how poorly she had worded her explanation and apologized quickly. "Of course not. Nothing like that. But surely you know that people are often different in social situations than in private—the nervousness, the pretenses. Everything comes into play, and I need to be prepared for it."

His eyes narrowed on her. "Do you do this for all your clients?"

"Well, no," she admitted, but held his gaze. "Most of my clients don't give me less than a month to find them a wife. We can't afford to make any mistakes, can we?"

Shane supposed she had a point, but he wasn't in the mood to see it. He had walked into her office, expecting a few minutes of idle chat, a signed contract, a check delivered and that would be that. In the past hour and a half she had probed him with personal questions, as much as assured him he was too stupid to know what he wanted, criticized his taste and even gotten him out of his pants—and under much less pleasant circumstances than he was accustomed to. This should have been as easy and impersonal as going to the bank. Instead, he felt as though he had just spent two hours in a doctor's office. And it wasn't over yet.

He glared at her. "I guess you're going to tell me what to wear?"

"Oh, no," she assured him. "I'll leave everything up to you. You can even pick the restaurant. I'm just an observer."

"This is the craziest thing I've ever heard of," he muttered.

"Believe me, it makes perfect sense. Would you accept a blind date from someone who didn't even know you? Same principle."

It wasn't the same at all, and for two cents Shane would have called the whole thing off right then. But he had made a deal, and despite what Jack said about things working differently in the civilized world, Shane Bartlett's word was still his bond.

Besides, he had gone this far. What harm could it do to give her one evening? At least he'd get a meal out of it.

He ran his hand through his hair and released a sigh. "Ah, what the hell," he decided ungraciously. "But not tonight,'' he interrupted as she opened her mouth for more instructions. ''I've left the pup locked up too long as it is and I'm not going to leave it alone again tonight.''

She looked surprised, and she was grinning. ''You really got a dog?''

Shane was unamused. ''Yes, I really got a dog. What's so funny about that?''

She chuckled and shook her head. ''Nothing,'' she answered, her eyes twinkling. ''It's just nice to know you follow instructions so well. This may be easier than I thought.''

Shane, as he stalked back to the dressing room, doubted that very much.

Four

———

You're going *out* with him?'' Emma exclaimed.

Cassie couldn't tell whether her expression indicated incredulity, disapproval or simple shock. The first rule Cassie had made when she took over the business was that no employee was ever allowed to date the clients. Since the only eligible men Cassie ever met were clients, she hadn't had a real date in almost five years.

''Before you let your imagination run away with you, it's not what you think.'' Cassie returned a file to the drawer and closed it. ''This is purely in the line of duty.''

Emma still looked doubtful, and Cassie gave her a reproving look. ''You know perfectly well this is too important to me to take any chances. How many matches have we made that fell apart on the first date because one or both of the parties was nervous, or trying too hard, or frankly, did a Jekyll and Hyde number on us the minute he got out of our sight? You can't be prepared for things like that unless you have up-close experience, and I am *not* going to let anything go wrong with Mr. Shane Bartlett. Besides," she gave a small shrug of her shoulders, "he doesn't seem too experienced at this kind of thing and could probably use a little polishing. First impressions are everything in this business, you know."

Emma nodded sagely, her expression perfectly bland. "Of course. You always have a perfectly reasonable explanation for everything you do. I should have known. And it doesn't have a thing to do with the fact that he's a well-set, very good-looking young man."

"Of course not." Cassie opened another drawer and thumbed through the files, her voice nonchalant. "Even if I weren't professional, he's not my type at all. You know that. This is strictly business. Besides—" she selected three folders and brought them over to Emma's desk "—he's not all that good-looking. Do a criteria scan on these three, will you?" she added as she saw the beginning of am impish smile playing in Emma's eyes. "We don't have much to go on yet, but we can start eliminating some possibilities."

"Are you leaving now?"

Cassie glanced at her watch. "I guess I have to. Shane is picking me up at seven. That's one thing he has going for him—some good old-fashioned manners. I offered to meet him at the restaurant, but he insisted on doing it right. Refreshing.''

Emma murmured, ''Hmm,'' in such a way that Cassie looked at her suspiciously. But Emma had already opened one folder and appeared absorbed in her work, her expression unrevealing.

Despite her blasé display of professionalism with Emma, Cassie couldn't put aside a nagging suspicion that there might be some truth in Emma's suggestion, and that bothered her. It had been bothering her, in fact, since yesterday when she had asked Shane out. It had seemed the perfectly logical thing to do at the time, but she wondered if she would have been so quick to see the logic in it with any other man. He still wasn't her type, but he *was* good-looking, and he had a kind of earthy charm that even she, in odd moments, found appealing. And he was interesting. Trying to decipher him was like peeling away the layers of a Chinese puzzle, and Cassie enjoyed a challenge. If she were completely honest with herself, she would have to admit she was looking forward to this evening. It might have been all in the line of duty, but sometimes there were fringe benefits.

And it *was* true: Shane Bartlett was the most important case to come across her desk since she had been in business. Everything depended on making him a successful match; she simply had to cover all the bases. By the time she was ready to introduce him to his perfect mate, all chances of error had to be completely eliminated. And if that meant sacrificing one evening of her time—or a dozen—so be it. She would do whatever she had to do.

Fluffy greeted her at the door with a great deal of purring and arching of her back. Against her better judgment, Cassie picked her up, stroked her and immediately started sneezing. With the cat in one hand and a tissue in the other, she went into the kitchen and filled the cat dish with dry food.

"There," she said, sniffing as Fluffy leaped for the dish. "That should keep you busy while I get dressed. All I need is cat fur in my eyes while I'm trying to put on makeup."

Shane had given her no indication as to where they were going—a mistake she would have to draw his attention to later—so she had no idea how to dress. His idea of an evening's entertainment could be anything from watching a wrestling match on television to a night of chili dogs and beer at the bowling alley. Not that her wardrobe included many choices. Warm-up suits, business suits and tennis shorts all started to look the same after a moment or two of staring at them, and it occurred to Cassie that with her newfound financial freedom she might at least have purchased a new dress. The only trouble was that she wasn't sure how long that freedom was going to last and she wasn't ready to splurge yet—not until she found Shane Bartlett a mate.

In the back of her closet, still covered by the dry cleaner's bag from its last trip out almost two years ago, was a simple black dress she had almost forgotten. It wasn't very businesslike with its plunging neckline, fitted torso and short skirt, but it would have to do. She could always cover her shoulders with a shawl.

She found herself experiencing a little tingle of excitement as she showered and changed. Cassie had almost forgotten how much she enjoyed getting dressed up. She brushed her hair vigorously over her head, shook it and let it fall into a fluffy aureole around her shoulders, smiling in surprised approval at her reflection in the mirror. "Not bad," she murmured. Of course, when she put her glasses on the effect was completely ruined, and in a moment of defiance she discarded the glasses for contact lenses. She would pay the price tomorrow, but tonight, at least, she would feel pretty.

Fluffy came in as she sat down at the dressing table to apply her makeup, and she spent the next twenty minutes alternately brushing cat hair off her black dress and trying to apply mascara with watery eyes. She was therefore somewhat behind schedule when the doorbell rang.

"Scoot!" She gave the cat a nudge, and Fluffy leaped off the dressing table and scampered toward the living room. Cassie gave her eyes a final dab with a tissue, applied a dusting of powder to her red nose and hurried after the cat to answer the front door.

Shane looked even better than she had imagined. The oyster-colored suit fitted as though it had been designed with only him in mind, the pale yellow shirt brought out the depth of his brown eyes and, she noticed, he was even wearing a tie. His dark curls were casually brushed, his boots were polished, and he carried his hat in his hand. The overall effect was of rugged masculinity barely tamed, nothing pretentious or overly done, everything completely natural. Shane was a man, she realized slowly, who didn't have to go to extraordinary lengths to impress a woman. All he had to do was stand there to take her breath away.

Cassie stepped back and let her eyes travel over him one more time. "You look..." Several superlatives sprang to mind, but she didn't want to overdo it. She settled for a simple, "Very nice."

"Thank you." He stepped inside, and she noticed for the first time that he was looking at her strangely, almost as though he wasn't sure he had the right apartment. "So do you." His eyes went from her loosened hair to the deep neckline of her dress to her bare knees, and when he raised his eyes to hers again, there was an unmistakable gleam of approval mixed with the surprise. "Different."

Cassie would have been less than a woman if the spark in his eyes hadn't generated a surge of satisfaction—even excitement—on her part. But she gave a casual toss of her head and explained with a shrug, "It's the contact lenses."

He brought his gaze from the way the black dress outlined her lower figure back to her face. "Oh, that's right. You were wearing glasses."

Cassie grinned and waved him toward the sofa. "Can you make yourself at home for a minute? I'm not quite ready. Do you want a drink?"

"No thanks. I made reservations at one of those swanky restaurants and I think you're supposed to be on time."

Cassie was impressed. "Okay, I'll just be a second. Have a seat."

Shane hadn't been looking forward to this evening. He hadn't dreaded it, exactly—not on par with the way

one might dread internment in a prison camp or tor-
ture by a mad scientist, for example—but he hadn't
expected it to be a picnic in the sun, either. Now, however, things were beginning to look up.

He hadn't give much thought to the possibility that
there might be a real woman lurking behind Cassie
Averil's thick glasses, tight bun and sensible shoes. If
she could change her personality as easily as she
changed her appearance, the evening might not be
quite the exercise in endurance he had anticipated. He
felt his sense of humor returning.

When Cassie came back, he was sitting on the sofa,
trailing a piece of yarn along the floor and grinning at
Fluffy's antic efforts to catch it. He got to his feet when
Cassie walked into the room. "Nice cat," he said,
"What's her name?"

"Fluffy. Do you like cats?"

"I like most things."

Cassie went over to the closet and took out a color-
ful fringed shawl. "Did you finish filling out the
form?"

Shane met her eyes and kept a straight face as he replied, "My dog ate it."

Cassie smiled sweetly. "No problem. I'll send you
another."

Shane took the shawl from her and draped it over
her shoulders, which surprised Cassie. He paused for
just a second longer with his hands on her shoulders,
then said, "That's nice. What is it?"

He was standing behind her, and Cassie had to twist
her head around to glance at him. That brought their
faces closer than she had expected, for he was bending

over her, and the brief quickening of her pulse startled her. "What?"

"Your perfume. It smells like lemon and vanilla."

"Oh." Cassie stepped away—casually, she hoped. "I'm afraid I forgot to put on any. That's just body lotion."

Shane smiled in a way that made her wish she had used a less descriptive term than "body lotion," but he said simply, "It's still nice."

Shane, she had noticed, was wearing no scent at all. He smelled like fresh air and clean cotton with just the faintest undertone of a spicy soap. It suited him.

She checked her evening purse for keys and wallet, then asked brightly, "Are you ready?"

"As ready as I'll ever be." He moved toward the door. Suddenly there was a loud screech, and Fluffy, her fur bristling, darted around Shane's ankles and hid under the table, her eyes gleaming red in the shadows. "God, I'm sorry!" Shane exclaimed. He knelt down on the floor and tried to coax Fluffy out from under the table. "She must've gotten under my feet. I guess I stepped on her."

Cassie chuckled. "Don't worry. You didn't hurt her. That's one of her little tricks to keep people from leaving."

Shane looked up dubiously. "Are you sure?"

"Positive. The minute we leave she'll be licking her fur and congratulating herself on how well she put you in your place." But Cassie thought his concern was admirable, even touching. Most men didn't like cats, and people who were good with animals were usually very good with women.

"Smart cat." Shane stood, a twinkle in his eye. "Must take after her mistress."

"I taught her everything she knows."

Shane chuckled and placed his hand lightly on her shoulder to escort her out. When they reached the front of the building, he took out his car keys. Cassie spotted the gleaming red Corvette parked next to her nondescript gray Honda and remarked, "Is that your car?"

"Uh-huh."

"Nice," she observed. "But next time rent a limo. You can afford it, and you should let your date know it. First impressions do make a difference."

He gave her an odd look as they started down the walk, and Cassie knew he wanted to argue. But he said instead, "You look sexy with your hair down."

Cassie repressed a self-satisfied smile. "I'm not your type."

"Right. Wrong color hair."

"And no bosom."

She caught his grin out of the corner of her eye as he opened the door for her. "Right."

But when Shane got behind the wheel and started the car, his expression grew thoughtful. "I like to drive. I don't want a limo. And I'm not looking for a gold digger, you know."

"That's exactly the problem," Cassie agreed. "The woman I find for you will have to be comfortable with wealth, or yours will intimidate her. And she should have some financial independence of her own, or she'll only be attracted to your money. But women who are accustomed to wealth will also be used to the luxuries it brings, which is why you may have to adapt your life-style a bit."

"I don't want to adapt my life-style. I told you before, I'm not going to change for anybody. I like myself the way I am."

"Everybody changes," Cassie pointed out patiently. "Everybody makes little compromises for other people. It's part of getting along. And no one is suggesting you pretend to be someone you're not. Just play the game a little, add a few flourishes. That's what you call romance."

He scowled. "I thought you didn't believe in romance."

"I don't. It's all part of the illusion. Dressing up for a date, sending flowers, hiring a limo and picking out an intimate little spot and a perfect champagne—window dressing and stage sets. Romance."

His tone was a little dry. "And that's all there is to it, huh?"

"Basically. Little gestures of consideration, proof that you're willing to go out of your way for the other person—that's how it starts."

"I'm not much for gestures. Seems to me things would be a lot simpler all the way around if people just did what came naturally. More honest."

"Honest isn't important at this stage of the game," Cassie assured him. "Illusion is."

He was silent for a while, apparently mulling that over. Then he said, "Flowers and limos, huh? That simple?"

"That simple."

"I'm not sure I like this."

"You promised to cooperate," she reminded him.

He looked as though he were regretting ever having made that promise.

Shane had done his homework, and the restaurant he had chosen did *not* serve nouvelle cuisine. But it was one of the classier gathering spots in Dallas; Cassie was impressed and she told him so.

"After this," he told her, "we're going to play miniature golf." Cassie's eyes widened in protest, and he laughed. His hand touched her shoulder lightly as he escorted her to the maître d's desk. "Come on, lady, just because I don't enjoy this sort of thing doesn't mean I don't know how to do it. Besides, this place has good food. Jack took me here when I first got into town. You know Jack Sanders, don't you?"

The maître d' showed them to their table, and she answered, "Yes. He and my assistant—you met Emma in the office—are old friends." The table was a good one, partially secluded but not too isolated, though whether that was by chance or prearrangement she didn't know. Cassie slipped her shawl off her shoulders, then said, "I've always liked Jack. It's a shame, though. An eligible bachelor like him, and he won't let me fix him up."

"Maybe he likes his freedom."

"Not that I can tell." Cassie accepted a menu from the maître d'; the wine list went to Shane, and he put it aside without a glance. "He's not much of a swinger."

Shane seemed surprised. "Oh, yeah? You could've fooled me. He's always trying to get me to go to some new club or check out some wild party. I thought that was the kind of thing he likes.''

Cassie laughed. "He may talk big, but he spends most of his nights at home with his sister or playing cards with Emma and her gray-haired friends. Sometimes he takes Emma to the movies." She shook her head regretfully. "I wish I could find a woman for him.''

"Fix him up with Emma," suggested Shane.

"Are you kidding?" Cassie reached across the table and retrieved the wine list. "I couldn't think of a worse match if I tried. They have nothing in common. They even argue about the movies they see. Jack likes to travel, Emma likes to stay at home. Emma reads, Jack watches television. Emma's afraid of horses and Jack raises them as a hobby. I could go on and on. It's a wonder they're even friends. I may not be one hundred percent perfect, but I do know better than to try to put those two together."

"It's nice to know you're not perfect," Shane murmured, but Cassie ignored him.

"Now," she said, "let me show you how to choose a wine.''

"I don't drink wine."

"Suppose your date does?"

"Then she can pick the wine.''

"A gentleman should know how to pick a wine. There's a very simple formula—"

"Everything's a formula with you, isn't it?"

"It keeps things simple. Now the thing to look for in wines is—"

"You've never been married, have you?"

Cassie looked up, a little surprised. "No."

"Small wonder," he muttered, and before she could question him he said, "If this is the way you're used to treating men, it's a wonder you can even get a date."

"This isn't a date," Cassie reiterated, though as hard as she tried not to, she bristled a little at his insult. "This is a business meeting and I'm trying to tell you—"

"No." He lifted one slim-fingered hand in protest. "Let me tell you something. A man doesn't like to be *told* everything, okay? He doesn't like to be corrected and criticized and watched like a bug on a glass every blessed minute of the day, and since you seem to know so much about how a woman likes to be treated, I thought you should know a little bit about how men like to be treated. It might help you out someday."

Cassie closed the wine list. "You don't want to learn how to pick out a wine."

His eyes were stubborn, his jaw set. "No."

She lifted one shoulder and put the wine list aside. A strained silence followed.

"Aren't you going to order wine?" Shane asked after a moment.

"Actually," Cassie admitted, "I can't drink wine. It gives me a headache." That made Shane chuckle, and Cassie relaxed. "I'm sorry," she said. "You were right. I shouldn't be giving you instructions. That defeats the whole purpose. I'll just sit here and watch."

Shane stifled a groan. "Then this is still an audition?"

"I wish you wouldn't think of it as that."

"Is there any chance we could just enjoy our meal like normal people?"

Cassie thought about that for a moment. "I don't see why not. Just act the same way you would on a real date."

"It's an audition," Shane said darkly.

The waiter arrived just then, sparing Cassie further discussion on the subject. Shane, predictably, ordered the biggest steak on the menu and draft beer. Cassie ordered vichyssoise, lobster Newburg and mineral water.

"It takes two, you know," Shane commented when the waiter was gone. "If I have to pretend this is a normal date, so do you."

"I'm not sure I remember how. It's been a long time since I had a real date."

"Now why doesn't that surprise me?" he murmured. When she looked at him sharply, he asked, "So why didn't you ever get married?"

Cassie should have responded that that was none of his business, that it was he who was being interviewed, not she, and that her motivations and marital status weren't at issue. But sometimes, she knew, the best way to get a man to talk about himself was to answer his questions, so she replied, "I chose not to. My career takes up all of my energy, and I like it that way."

He nodded with a perception that she thought was uncharacteristic of him. "It's easier to fix up other people's lives than your own."

"What about you? Why do you *want* to get married so desperately?"

"It's not desperation." The waiter brought their drinks, and he took a sip of his beer. "It's just something I've always known I wanted. It's like being complete—everything is empty unless there's a family to share it with."

"Ego," she observed, nodding. "Reflected glory. A wife, a big house and lots of little kiddies to carry on the great name."

He gave her a look of barely repressed distaste. "You sure have a sour way of looking at things. It just so happens I like kids. I always have. I grew up with a bunch of them, remember?"

Cassie remembered, and felt somewhat chastened as she imagined him playing big brother to a houseful of orphans.

"I like them when they're small and I like them when they're bigger," he told her. "I like teaching them things and watching them grow up. I'd make a good father," he finished confidently.

Cassie imagined that he would.

"What about you?" he asked. "Don't you ever think about having a family?"

"Not really." In fact, she had thought about it a lot when she was younger, but her own goals and ambitions had gotten in the way, and somehow, over the years, her romantic notions about fulfillment and procreation had lost their sheen. That seemed rather sad in a way. "I like my life the way it is."

"How old are you?"

"Too old for you."

"Pardon?"

"I'm almost thirty years old," she replied. "My childbearing years are spinning out like a clock in fast motion. And you should be saving your questions for someone who at least has a chance of giving the right answers."

He grinned ruefully and shook his head. "You don't cut a guy any slack at all, do you?"

Cassie merely smiled as her soup and his salad were served.

He watched her taste her soup. "What is that?"

"Vichyssoise," she explained. "It's kind of a cold potato soup."

"Like potato salad?"

She laughed. "Not exactly." She hesitated, then offered, "Would you like to taste it?"

"Are you allowed to do that in a place like this?"

Cassie's eyes sparkled as she pushed the bowl across the table to him. "Not really," she confided. "But in this case we'll make an exception."

Shane picked up his own spoon and tasted the soup cautiously. He looked surprised. "That's not bad. I think I'll have some."

He beckoned the waiter and ordered a bowl of vichyssoise, and while he was waiting for it to be delivered, he finished his salad. Cassie watched him in amusement. Any doubts she'd had about his ability to conduct himself with ease and assurance in a social setting were completely erased, and she couldn't understand why he had led her to believe he was awkward about such things. Being with him was natural and unconstrained, his conversation was direct and effortless, and—except for the times when he was glaring at her with that familiar stubborn set to his jaw—he was fun to be with. A man with his kind of guileless charm should have had no difficulty at all getting a date.

Getting a wife, of course, was another matter entirely.

As the main course was served, he told entertaining stories about his adventures in Alaska and made occasional intriguing references to his early years growing up in group homes in Washington State. All of it was related with a touch of humor and not a trace of pathos, which Cassie found fascinating. Shane Bartlett appeared to be one of those rare people who could turn almost any situation to his advantage, merely by expecting the best to happen and allowing no room in his plans for failure.

"So, anyway," he said, "I didn't have anything else to spend my money on all those years, so I started putting it into oil. A little bit here, a little there. Next thing I knew I was a major holder in a company that was a lot bigger than I ever expected it to be. Shortly after that this big consortium came along and bought us out, and here I am."

Cassie shook her head slowly. "Amazing," she murmured.

"What? My Cinderella story?" He scraped the last of his baked potato from the skin.

"That," agreed Cassie, "and the fact that you've managed to finish a soup, salad, the biggest steak I've ever seen and all the trimmings without even stopping for breath. Where do you put it all?"

He grinned. "You know what they say about orphans: they're always hungry. Ready for dessert?"

Cassie groaned.

On a scale of one to ten, Shane had planned for this evening to be, at best, a three. So far the score had passed seven and was steadily climbing. It was, in fact, one of the nicest times he had ever had just having dinner with a woman, and Shane didn't really understand why. It had something to do with the fact that Cassie Averil was easy to talk to, which surprised him; even when he was irritated with her, he was always looking forward to what she would do or say next. She kept him thinking, and didn't let him get away with anything, something Shane couldn't help admiring her for. She was different from the women he had known, and he enjoyed the puzzle even if he didn't always enjoy the differences. If the women she fixed him up with were as interesting as she was, perhaps this whole business wouldn't be so difficult, after all.

"So, Cassie," he said, leaning back as the waiter began to clear the table. It was easier to call her Cassie when her hair was down. "How am I doing so far?"

Her eyes had a nice sparkle in the candlelight, and the edge of her smile was a little impish. Shane had never seen eyes so green before, nor had he realized what an attractive color that was.

"All right," she answered. "In fact, very nicely. I'm having a good time."

"Good. Then you can pay for the meal."

She laughed, and Shane liked that, too. He always felt he had scored a small victory when he made her laugh.

All in all, he decided, she was an attractive woman—not his type, of course, but she did have a certain allure. He liked the way her hair brushed her shoulders and that dress made him forget he had always been attracted to more well-endowed women. She wore a locket necklace that rested just a fraction of an inch above the cleavage of her dress, and all night his eyes had been straying to that particular portion of her anatomy. More than once he had resisted the urge to reach across the table and take the locket in his fingers—and not because he was particularly interested in lockets, either. He supposed that was why women wore necklaces like that with low-cut gowns; to drive men crazy with wanting to touch.

"Have you ever been in love?" he asked impulsively.

She looked startled. "What a strange question."

"Not really. You're supposed to be handling my love life. I'd like to know what qualifications you have."

She looked slightly annoyed, but answered, "First of all, I've told you love is an ambiguous term. Secondly, of course, I've been in love—dozens of times."

Now he was curious. "And?"

"And what?" She gave a dismissing shrug. "That 'being in love' feeling is just a chemical reaction, a flare of so-called passion that burns itself out. It's not really important."

"What do you mean, it's not important? You don't expect me to marry someone I'm not in love with, do you?"

A look of mild exasperation mixed with puzzlement came into her eyes. "You're being inconsistent. Do you realize that? If you really believed all that romantic nonsense about instant passion and love sickness, you wouldn't have come to me to order a wife. You would have just waited around for the magic to strike, right? But you're sensible, just like I am. You know it takes more than chemistry to make a match.''

Shane felt as though he should have an answer to that, and it disturbed him that he didn't. Fortunately the pastry cart arrived just then, so he didn't have to think about it for long. But he couldn't help wondering what it would take to make a woman like Cassie Averil believe in the power of passion.

After dinner they walked for a while in the city lights, and Shane was somewhat subdued. Cassie found his silence comfortable, just as the evening had been. Simple, unstrained, enjoyable. It occurred to her to wonder, briefly, whether she was responding solely to the pleasure of being out with a handsome man—he had, indeed, made heads turn in the restaurant—or whether it was Shane's company that had made the evening so memorable. She decided it was both.

He drove her home and walked her to her door. "So," he said as Cassie took out her keys, "do I get a final report?"

Cassie smiled to herself. The night had been so pleasant that she had almost forgotten the original purpose of the evening. "I would say... very good. A B plus."

"I guess you took off points for romantic gestures."

"Well, you can always work on those."

"I'll do that."

She inserted the key into the lock and turned to him. "I'll send you another profile form," she reminded him. "Fill it out as soon as possible."

"The truth is," he said, ignoring her, "it wasn't really a fair test. I mean, I knew up front it was only a make-believe date, and you didn't get to judge me on my best stuff."

Cassie hadn't realized until then how close he was standing, and there was an oddly thoughtful, almost mischievous glint in his eyes. "Like what?" she inquired a little suspiciously.

"Like this." He took her in his arms and kissed her.

If Cassie had to put the experience into words, she would have likened it to the time she had been playing in the surf at Galveston and had been caught off guard by a breaker that had crashed over her head and sent her sweeping to shore. It had been shocking, unexpected, and had taken her breath away and swept her along faster than she cared to go. But she was helpless against the impact—helpless and exhilarated.

Her pulse soared and her skin flared with fever as his warmth encircled her, strong hands cupping her shoulder blades and pressing her close. His kiss was sure and thorough, promising but not demanding, overwhelming in its pure sensuality. Her muscles weakened and her breath stopped and every nerve ending in her body responded to him with a tingling ache that left her senseless. Chemistry, she thought dizzily. Only chemistry...

The kiss ended slowly, and with the same thorough care with which it had begun. Long after he had lifted his face she could still taste him, still feel the slight scratchiness of his cheek against hers. She rested her hands against his arms for support and could feel his breath against her hair, his eyes upon her. She didn't look at him, because it took far longer than it should have to compose herself.

At last she put her hand against his chest and stepped away. She looked up at him and smiled. "Don't ever try to seduce a girl on the first date," she advised pleasantly. "It's bad form and shows you're in a hurry. I'll be in touch with you in a couple of days," she added as she opened the door. "Meanwhile, don't forget the form. Good night."

The last thing she saw was his startled expression, and then she closed the door and leaned against it heavily. Her legs were still trembling.

One thing was certain: Shane Bartlett didn't need any instructions in the fine art of the good-night kiss.

Five

___

The next day Cassie's eyes were red-rimmed and swollen from the contact lenses, and she couldn't get a thing done at work for thinking about Shane. Emma asked tactful, borderline businesslike questions about the "date," and Cassie suspected the other woman knew she was being evasive with her answers. But what could Cassie say? She wasn't even sure *she* knew what to think anymore.

Shane Bartlett was without doubt one of the most contradictory, complex and outrageous men she had ever met. He claimed to be uncomfortable on dates, yet he had flirted with her as naturally as he drew breath. Despite the fact that she had made the terms of the evening clear from the outset, he had somehow managed to turn it into a real date. Of course, he'd had no right to kiss her, but she hadn't exactly hit him over the head with her purse for trying, had she?

And therein lay the problem. There was something about him—about simply being with him—that made Cassie feel like a woman, and she hadn't known that feeling for a long time. She was very much afraid of losing her objectivity.

She made a halfhearted effort to go through the files of some women Emma had recommended as possible matches for Shane Bartlett. But she couldn't really concentrate. Every time she brought up a mental picture of a woman in a file she imagined Shane kissing her. And every time she did *that* she grew more irritated with herself. She kept expecting Shane to call, or walk through the door, and the expectation was tinged with excitement, like that of a teenager waiting for an invitation to the prom. That irritated her even more.

She left the office early and arrived home disgruntled, snappish and thoroughly disgusted with herself. Fluffy had apparently used the cat door to explore the call of the wild, and the apartment was empty, which didn't improve her mood any.

"I don't know why I got a cat, anyway," she grumbled, bending to pick up the mail from the floor. "All she's good for is making me sneeze and running up the grocery bill."

The mail included several bills, an advertisement for life insurance and a postcard from her parents, who were vacationing on Saint Thomas. "Why would anyone want to go to Saint Thomas when they live in Florida?" she muttered ungraciously. "It's too hot there this time of year, anyway."

She was still staring with well-disguised envy at the picture of clear Caribbean waters and quaint red-roofed cottages when the doorbell rang. She thought it was just surprise that caused her pulse to jump, but when she walked quickly to the door she was half expecting—or perhaps hoping—to see Shane.

A man in a florist's cap stood there with a long white box in his arm. He checked the card. "Miss—" he looked at the card again "—Fluffy Averil?"

Cassie blinked. "I beg your pardon?"

"I've got a delivery here for Miss Fluffy Averil," he insisted more assertively. "Will you sign?"

"Oh . . . sure." A little dazed, she initialed the form and accepted the box.

As soon as she closed the door, she tore off the card and opened it quickly. Across the top was scrawled, "A romantic gesture." And beneath it was written: "Dear Fluffy. I'm sorry I stepped on your tail. S."

Cassie opened the box. Inside were a dozen long-stemmed roses.

She laughed. She hugged the roses to her and laughed until her knees gave way and she sank to the floor. Then she started to sneeze, and that only made her laugh harder.

Cassie was also allergic to roses.

The weekend passed and Cassie used the time to good advantage by giving herself a stern lecture on the importance of maintaining her perspective. Shane Bartlett was sweet, entertaining and blatantly sensual; he was also stubborn, opinionated and more than a little chauvinistic. He was, in short, the best and the

Look what we've got for you:

... A FREE 20k gold electroplate chain
... plus a sampler set of 4 terrific Silhouette
Desire® novels, specially selected by our
editors.

... PLUS a surprise mystery gift
that will delight you.

All this just for trying our Reader Service!

If you wish to continue in the Reader Service,
you'll get 6 new Silhouette Desire® novels every
month—before they're available in stores. That's
SNEAK PREVIEWS for just $2.24* per book—
26¢ less than the cover price—plus only 69¢
postage and handling for the entire shipment!

Plus There's More!

With your monthly book shipments, you'll also get our newsletter, packed
with news of your favourite authors and upcoming books—FREE! And as
a valued reader, we'll be sending you additional free gifts from time to
time—as a token of our appreciation for being a home subscriber.

THERE IS NO CATCH. You're not required to buy a single book, ever. You
may cancel Reader Service privileges anytime, if you want. All you have to
do is write "cancel" on your statement or simply return your shipment of
books to us at our cost. The free gifts are yours anyway. It's a super-sweet
deal if ever there was one. Try us and see!

Get 4 FREE full-length Silhouette Desire® novels.

Plus

this lovely 20k gold electroplate chain

Plus

a surprise free gift

▼ PLUS LOTS MORE! MAIL THIS CARD TODAY ▼

Silhouette's Best-Ever "Get Acquainted" Offer

PLACE STICKER FOR 6 FREE GIFTS HERE

Yes, I'll try Silhouette books under the terms outlined on the opposite page. Send me 4 free Silhouette Desire® novels, a free electroplated gold chain and a free mystery gift.

326 CIS 8155 (C-S-D-03/90)

NAME _____

ADDRESS _____ APT. _____

CITY _____

PROV. _____ POSTAL CODE _____

PRINTED IN U.S.A.

Don't forget...

... Return this card today and receive 4 free books, free electroplated gold chain and free mystery gift.

... You will receive books before they're available in stores.

... No obligation to buy. You can cancel at any time by writing "cancel" on your statement or returning a shipment to us at our cost.

If offer card is missing, write to: Silhouette Books®
P.O. Box 609, Fort Erie, Ontario L2A 5X3

**Business
Reply Mail**

No Postage Stamp
Necessary if Mailed
in Canada

Postage will be paid by

Silhouette® Books
P.O. Box 609
Fort Erie, Ontario
L2A 9Z9

worst of all that was male, and he had employed her to find his match. It was imperative that she do so without allowing her personal impressions—good or bad—to cloud her judgment. More than her professional reputation was at stake; her very livelihood depended on her doing the best job of her life for Shane Bartlett.

On Monday she turned the other clients over to Emma and cloistered herself in her office, dedicating her full attention to Shane Bartlett. She wrote down everything she knew about him, cataloged the information and applied several standard psychological tests. The tests would be more accurate when his profile form arrived, but for now she had enough to begin with. By Wednesday it became obvious that the form wasn't going to arrive, and she squared her shoulders and intensified the search.

On Friday afternoon she rushed from her office, dropped a file on Emma's desk and exclaimed triumphantly. "Mindy Howard!"

Emma looked dubious. "For Mr. Bartlett?"

"Of course! She's new money—her family was strictly blue-collar until her mother remarried, so she's got all those down-to-earth values Shane thinks are so important. She just turned twenty-three, and I happen to know her mother wants her to get married in the worst way...."

"I don't know." A small ridge of concern appeared between Emma's brows. "We haven't had much luck with her in the past. She seems a little...eager to me."

"That's because she's young," Cassie replied airily. "All young people are eager. And on my time schedule, eagerness is a plus. She still has blond hair, doesn't she? Get her on the phone and see. And if she doesn't," Cassie added, hurrying back to her office, "tell her to get to the beauty parlor this afternoon. I'm going to call Shane."

She paused at the door and lifted her crossed fingers. "This could be it, Emma. We're on our way!"

She didn't notice that Emma didn't share her enthusiasm. Too much was at stake for Cassie to risk pessimism now.

"Are you sure?" Jack asked. "We could fly up to Vegas in my plane, gamble the night away and be back by tomorrow afternoon."

"I'm sure," Shane said into his mobile phone as he picked up a tennis ball, rolled it along the ground and watched as the puppy skittered around the slick surface of the pool trying to catch it. "I don't feel like going anywhere this weekend. Besides, what would I do with the dog?"

"Hell, take him with you. We'll put him in the presidential suite at the MGM Grand."

Shane chuckled, leaned back in the webbed chair and stretched his bare legs out in the sun. "No thanks. Gambling's a vice, and you ought to know better. When are you going to start acting your age and settle down?"

"When they bury me, son. When they bury me. Speaking of which, how's it going with the matchmaker?"

Shane frowned. Lately that was his reaction whenever Cassie Averil crossed his mind. "I think your matchmaker's a nut," he said without qualification. "You know what she told me? There's no such thing as love, she said. She calls herself a matchmaker. I mean, she's dealing with people's lives here, and she doesn't even believe in romance. She thinks she can fix people up just like you'd separate oranges from apples. How'd she ever get into this business in the first place?"

"Well, now, that sounds mighty funny coming from you. You're the one who thought all it took to find a wife was making up your mind."

Shane's frown deepened. Cassie had said something similar, and he still didn't like the implication. Maybe he had gone about the whole thing a little forcefully, but he had never been as clinical as Cassie Averil was. He hadn't really expected to just meet a woman and marry her. He knew there had to be some courtship involved, some romance, some falling in love. The only thing he had been cloudy on was *how* that was supposed to happen, and he supposed what disturbed him most now was the fact that he had never given much thought to how complicated the whole process could be.

"I just didn't expect her to be so coldhearted," he said, and he was thinking about what had happened after he had kissed her. She had responded to him. He had felt the layers of ice melting away and turning to steam, and for a moment kissing her had been the single most exciting, absorbing and fulfilling experience of his life. And then there she was with her schoolteacher's smile, closing the door in his face. A man didn't forget a thing like that.

"Cassie Averil isn't coldhearted," Jack said. "She's just got her own way of doing things. Wait till you get to know her. You'll see."

The puppy had pushed the tennis ball into the pool, and Shane got up to retrieve it. "Maybe I don't want to get to know her. Who needs that kind of trouble? As far as I'm concerned—"

The telephone beeped in his ear. Shane held it away from his face and scowled. Of all the modern conveniences that awaited him when he returned to civilization, Call Waiting was his least favorite. "Wait a minute. It's probably another salesman with some great swampland in Florida."

"Take it," Jack advised. "With your luck the coastline will probably shift and you'll end up owning beachfront property. I'll hold."

Shane grinned and depressed the button. It was Cassie Averil, and he couldn't believe the way his heart started beating a little faster when he heard her voice. "Well," he drawled, "fancy hearing from you."

"I've got some good news for you, I think." Her voice sounded pleasant and professional, but he thought he detected a trace of breathlessness. When he pictured her in his mind, it was with her hair down and a gold locket lying between her breasts. "I've found someone I'd like you to meet. I think you two could be perfect for each other."

"Oh, yeah? Tell me about her."

"It's usually better if I do that in person. Could you come into the office this afternoon?"

There was nothing Shane would have liked better than to see her today, even if it was to discuss another woman. But some perversity, solely generated by the memory of their last encounter, caused him to reply, "I can't today. How about tomorrow?"

She hesitated. "Tomorrow's Saturday."

"No problem. Why don't you drive out here and we'll go for a swim. You can tell me all about her between laps."

A note of stubbornness came into her own voice. "I have to do my laundry on Saturday."

"Sunday, then. That's better, anyway. The construction crew won't be here. Less noise."

Again there was a long silence. "I was hoping you'd be able to meet her this weekend."

It gave Shane a devilish sense of satisfaction to suggest, "You could bring her along."

"I'll see you Sunday. Alone."

"Good. I sleep late on Sundays, so not before noon, okay? And don't forget to bring your suit."

She hung up. Shane depressed the button again, grinning broadly. "Guess who that was?" he asked Jack.

Sunday dawned clear and hot, perfect for a pool party. Cassie was unimpressed. Though she had to admit a certain curiosity about the way Shane lived, she had no intention of turning the afternoon into a party of any sort. She was still a little irritated with him for postponing the meeting for two days, anyway. He was the one who had set the month deadline, not she. And now he was acting as though he didn't care whether she made it or not. Or perhaps he was simply trying to make her job more difficult, which wouldn't surprise her in the least.

Well, she wasn't going to play his game. She would go out there, because that was part of her job, but she wouldn't stay any longer than was absolutely necessary. Nor did she have any intention of letting this turn into a social occasion.

But she spent an inordinate amount of time standing before her closet, wishing she had something new to wear. She pulled out a pair of shorts, but decided they weren't at all appropriate attire for a business meeting. The gray suit was stifling on a day like this, and not even for Shane Bartlett would she force herself to wear business clothes on a Sunday. She practically ripped the suit off in disgust and left it lying in a pile on the floor.

She tried on a pair of linen slacks and a silk blouse, which was technically perfect for the occasion. She found a dozen things wrong with it. The long-sleeved blouse was too hot, the slacks needed pressing, the colors made her look washed out. The truth was, the outfit simply wasn't feminine enough. It was Sunday; she had a right to look feminine if she wanted, didn't she?

Wasting no more time on debate, she stepped into a cotton sundress with a low, square neckline and a long, full skirt. The last time she had worn it had been at a barbecue given by one of her clients; there was simply no room in her everyday life for something as playful as a sundress. But it was cool, it was flattering, and it was casual. She didn't want Shane Bartlett to think she had gone to any particular trouble on his behalf.

Not daring to look in the mirror lest she change her mind, Cassie gathered her hair in a ponytail and glanced at her watch. It was already past noon. She gave Fluffy a quick scratch behind the ears, picked up Mindy Howard's file and left the apartment.

Five seconds later she returned, hurried back to the bedroom and stuffed her swimsuit in her purse. She left without looking back.

The drive took over half an hour, and Cassie couldn't understand why anyone would choose to live so far out of town unless he intended to raise livestock, which Shane had positively assured her over dinner that he didn't. Mindy Howard professed a love for country living, but Cassie had never seen the appeal.

She saw the stone gates of Long Acre and turned left onto a drive that wound for half a mile before the house even came into view. Along the way she noticed fenced in meadows empty of cattle, a shimmering pond occupied by two ducks, and smooth green fields stretching away on either side. She had to admit that it was pretty.

The area around the big brick house was littered with construction debris and piles of earth, and the place looked deserted. There was a construction trailer off to the side, sheltered by the shade of a big oak, and she went there first. No one answered her knock, or her call. She left the trailer and looked around curiously.

The sound of laughter reached her, accompanied by splashing and a background drift of music. He *was* having a party. And all this time she had pictured him wasting away in solitude out here in the middle of nowhere. She should have known better; men were all alike.

Mastering her dismay, she followed the sounds of poolside fun around the house, across a flagstone patio and through a sheltered courtyard until it opened on a turquoise-tiled, kidney-shaped pool. Plush-cushioned longue chairs were arranged in the sun, and a radio, tuned to a golden oldies station, was set up on a picnic table next to a big cooler. At the edge of the pool Shane pushed a beach ball back and forth between himself and a small brown-and-white puppy, who was paddling madly to keep his head above water and yipping happily whenever the ball came his way.

An indulgent smile tugged her lips as Cassie watched, and she couldn't deny the wave of tender amusement that swept her. How could anyone *not* like this man?

Shane saw her then and waved. He caught the puppy under one arm and lifted himself out of the water, causing the maternal affection Cassie had felt while watching him play to turn quickly to something else.

He was wearing a pair of small red briefs that clung to his pelvis like a second skin. Water smoothed the dark hair on his legs and chest into a molded pattern that followed the bronzed contours of his muscles. His hips were narrow, his legs were long and his chest was lean and well defined. His entire body was so... bare. Wow, Cassie thought to herself dazedly.

She was startled out of her absorption when a wet ball of fur hit her ankles.

"Sorry," Shane called. He snapped his fingers. "Whiskers, come here."

The dog ignored him, leaping excitedly up and down on Cassie's toes. To hide the sudden color in her cheeks, Cassie bent to pet the puppy, who immediately stopped jumping and shook himself, splattering Cassie's dress and sunglasses with water.

Shane laughed. "I told you to bring your swimsuit." He picked up a towel and dried his face as he came over to her. "Come here, you mutt."

He knelt beside her, and Cassie, who was wiping the water droplets off her glasses, had a blurred impression of tanned knees and muscular thighs. She quickly put her glasses back on so that she could see, but by that time Shane had scooped up the puppy and was standing. He set the puppy down in the direction of the grassy courtyard and sent it off to play with a pat. Then he turned back to Cassie. "Glad to see you found the place."

"Oh, sure." She got to her feet. "I've lived in Dallas all my life, and the Bureau of Tourism requires that every resident know the name and location of all the big ranches so that we can brag to outsiders. Fluffy thanks you for the roses, by the way."

"I'm glad she liked them. Do you think she'll marry me?"

"I'm afraid she's not your type, either. Too independent."

He grinned and draped the towel around his neck. "You look pretty today."

He shouldn't have been surprised, but he was. The sundress was simple and feminine, and he liked the way an occasional breeze lifted it at the hem and curved it around her calves. The ponytail was girlish and casual, and the sunshine brought a blush to her skin that he had never noticed before. Every time he saw her she looked different, and the differences were always welcome. A man would never grow bored with a woman as full of surprises as she was.

"Thanks," she said. A dimple formed at the corner of her mouth. "You don't look too bad yourself."

"What, this old thing?" He gestured toward his briefs. "Just a little something I slipped on."

"Very little," agreed Cassie. For a moment they just stood there, smiling at each other, and then Cassie turned to look around. "Nice house. Jack did a good job."

"I told him what I wanted, and he somehow managed to get it all strung together. I guess I wasn't one of his easiest clients."

"Having worked with you, I can agree with that."

He moved to slip on a short-sleeved denim shirt, discarding the towel. "Just like I told you, I know what I want. It's still a mess inside, but I'll show you around if you like."

Cassie didn't hesitate to accept his offer, feeling certain that the design of his house would reflect the man . . . and hoping it would help her to understand him.

He took her around the pool and through a set of wide French doors, warning her to be careful of the loose lumber and sawhorses scattered about. The puppy squeezed past her and left his own set of muddy footprints in the wake of the large wet ones Shane tracked across the dusty tile.

They stood inside a large, airy kitchen that boasted glass-fronted cabinets, a big center work island and a vaulted ceiling. Spaces had been left for the appliances, and the countertops were a rich royal blue. Three steps down led to a dining area that overlooked the pool. Adjacent to that, through a set of swinging doors, was a formal dining room, and off the dining room was a barbecue patio with a minikitchen and room for all the accoutrements. Cassie couldn't help smiling to herself. It figured that a large portion of Shane's house would be given over to the business of eating.

They circled through the dining room, went up three more steps and came into the main part of the house. The family room featured a cathedral ceiling, a mammoth fieldstone fireplace and a glass wall with a commanding view of the rich green meadows beyond. The walls were stucco, and a loft encircled the room on three sides.

"What a wonderful room," Cassie said in an awed tone as she approached the window. "I'd never get tired of looking at this view."

"Me, either. It feels like you can see forever out that window, doesn't it?"

Shane placed his hand lightly upon her shoulder as he stood beside her, and it was such a natural, companionable gesture that neither of them felt awkward standing close together and sharing the view. Cassie began to appreciate some of the advantages of living in the country.

"This is really great," she said, turning to survey the room again. Shane dropped his hand. "Big but cozy at the same time. I can picture it with chintz furniture arranged in little conversation groups, dried flower arrangements, maybe some cushions on the floor..."

"I picture big leather furniture and Navaho pottery."

Cassie started to argue, but remembered it wasn't her house and none of her business. She smiled ruefully. "The difference between men and women, I guess. Are you going to have a decorator in?"

"Jack says I have to. That's another reason I need a wife. What do I know about drapes and tables and slipcovers and such?"

"It's cheaper in the long run to hire a decorator."

He grinned. "But not nearly as much fun." He placed his hand on her back and continued the tour. "Over here is a game room and an exercise room with a real sauna and whirlpool. Off the exercise room is an indoor pool. It's not as big as the other one, of course, but it'll be nice to have if it ever does get cold."

They went up a flight of inner stairs and emerged in the shelf-lined loft. Cassie's imagination was racing with the possibilities for that loft—how she would decorate the shelves and arrange small reading and napping areas in the recesses. She thought a potted tree would look nice under the skylight, and even Shane liked that idea.

He showed her the master bedroom with its dais for the bed, its huge walk-in closets and its sunken tub and Jacuzzi. There was a balcony off the bedroom that, for the moment, overlooked a mound of earth, but which Shane told her would soon be transformed into a flower garden. Cassie could imagine her taking her coffee out onto the balcony every morning, inhaling the dewy, flower-scented air and watching the sun rise. What kind of man would think of planting a flower garden beneath his bedroom window? A very unusual one, she decided.

He took her through more bedrooms and baths than she could count, showed her the view from every window and took her down a wide, curving staircase that opened onto an expansive foyer.

"If I have a daughter," he said, standing at the bottom of the stairs and looking back up, "she'll come down these stairs in a long white dress with the guests lined up from here to here." He gestured from the foyer to the great room opposite. "This is a great house for a wedding, don't you think?"

"Even your own," she pointed out.

"Yeah," he agreed, smiling. "I'd like that."

"So." He turned to her. "What do you think?"

"About the house?"

He nodded.

There seemed to be a touch of genuine anxiety in his expression, as though her opinion really mattered. Cassie smiled. "I think it's perfect. Peaceful, comfortable, larger than life—just like you. I think," she added, "that your wife will be a very lucky woman." And, she thought to herself, for more reasons than were apparent in this spacious, custom-built home and the financial freedom it implied. It was the man whose thoughtful attention had gone into planning a place for his family who was the real prize.

They exited by the front door and Shane pointed out the landscaping he was planning, the most important of which, and obviously the most well thought out, was the children's play yard. The little boy that lingered in Shane was revealed as he enthusiastically described tunnels and rope swings, wooden forts and jungle gyms and an electric train that would carry its pint-size passengers from one part of the yard to the other.

Cassie laughed. "You must've spent the past six months with your head buried in an enormous toy catalog."

"I know," he agreed ruefully. "I'm running out of places to put all the stuff I want to buy."

Cassie chuckled and slipped her arm through his. "You're a funny man. Nice, but funny."

He looked a little surprised at her gesture, and his eyes went to her hand, looped through the crook of his elbow. But before she could draw away or regret the impulsive display of affection, his hand covered hers securely, holding it in place, and he responded smugly, "Thank you. I do my best."

They crossed the courtyard and came upon the pool again. The puppy, exhausted from exploring, lay down under a chair and was fast asleep in a matter of seconds. Cassie spared a brief moment of envy for the small animal's carefree life; it was Sunday, after all, and there was nothing she would have liked better than to stretch out in the sun and relax. But she had come here on business and she determinedly brought her mind back to the job at hand.

"Well," she said briskly, perching on the edge of a longue chair and pulling the file from her purse. "Let me tell you about Mindy Howard."

"Who?" Shane opened the cooler, pulled out a bottle of beer, then glanced at her curiously.

"The girl I've found for you. Mindy Howard."

"Do you want one of these?"

"No thanks."

He opened one anyway and brought it over to her, and Cassie tried not to be annoyed with his apparent lack of interest. She also tried not to be distracted by his lean brown thighs as he sat in the chair facing her, dangling his own bottle of beer by the neck between his knees.

"Mindy," she began, "is twenty-three and very sweet. She's from Oklahoma originally and was raised on a farm. Her stepfather is a troubleshooter for one of the big companies in town, so they have money. But they don't have too much and they haven't had it for long. Mindy's a little bit shy around the big wheeler-dealers her stepfather associates with, and I guess you could say she's not really used to the glamorous life yet. She's been brought up to believe that the home and family are all-important, so I think you have something in common there. Here's a picture of her."

Shane took the snapshot and studied it, and though Cassie watched carefully for some change of expression, there was none. "She's cute," he said after a moment, and returned the photograph to her. "I thought you said you didn't keep pictures of your clients."

"I said," Cassie corrected, "that we didn't keep photographs for browsing. Naturally people want to see a photo before they go out with someone."

"What about me? You don't have a picture of me."

She gave him a meaningful look. "If you had bothered to complete your form, you would have noticed instructions regarding obtaining a photograph."

He shrugged and took a swig of his beer.

Cassie went on determinedly. "Mindy is very easy to get along with. Feminine and charming and a good listener. She doesn't have particularly extravagant tastes and she's not very demanding." The more she spoke, the duller Mindy sounded. Or was Cassie merely trying to make her sound dull for reasons of her own? How clouded had she allowed her judgment to get where Shane was concerned? Suddenly confused, Cassie consulted the form. "She says here that her life's ambition is—"

"Do you really have to read all that?"

"Well, no. It's just that—"

"Good." Shane leaned back and stretched his legs out so that his bare ankles almost brushed hers. Cassie quickly shifted her legs the other way. "I think it would be more fun to find out some of this stuff on my own."

"This will go much more smoothly," Cassie insisted, "if you both know something about each other from the start. Then you'll have a foundation, a basis for—"

"I'd rather do it the old-fashioned way." He seemed bored and anxious to move on. "So when do I meet her?"

Cassie closed the file, hoping he showed more enthusiasm when he met Mindy than he was showing now. "I'll make the arrangements, if that's okay. Sometime next week?"

"Sure." He took another sip of beer. "All finished?"

Reluctantly Cassie put the file back into her purse. Somehow she had expected this to take longer, and she wasn't looking forward to the long drive back into town. It had been pleasant, sitting for a few moments with the warmth of the sun on her back and the smell of chlorine in the air, watching light dance off the turquoise water...and being with Shane. It was the way a Sunday should be.

She stood, hitching the strap of her purse over her shoulder, and extended her hand to him in a very businesslike manner. "Well, then, I'll be in touch, all right?"

He ignored her offered hand and lifted a gaze to her that was lazy and sun-crinkled. "Don't you ever relax?"

"I beg your pardon?"

"Take the day off, sit around and do nothing, maybe even forget about work for a while. Don't you ever do that?"

She shook her head ruefully. "Not very often," she admitted, although he could have no idea how tempting the suggestion sounded.

"Today might be a good time to start. Do you have a date waiting for you at home?"

She blinked, startled. "Why, no."

He smiled. "Did you bring your swimsuit?"

Cassie hesitated. The crystal-clear water beckoned, the sun sparkled on the tiled deck, and the frosty droplets condensed on her untasted bottle of beer. This was so unprofessional. She shouldn't even be considering it.

She looked at Shane. "Yes, as a matter of fact I did."

He grinned. "You can change in the trailer."

After a moment she returned his grin and walked off toward the trailer.

Six

___

You're very seductive. Do you know that?"

For a moment Shane couldn't reply. He was entirely too busy noticing the way the shiny green maillot suit clung to her figure as she walked toward him, and the way her slim legs seemed to go on forever. Once he had thought bikinis were sexy, but he would be hard put to find anything more alluring than the way Cassie Averil looked in that emerald one-piece with the sun painting streaks of copper and gold in her hair.

He let out a cautious breath. "*I* am?"

She sat on the edge of a chair to remove her sandals and sunglasses. Shane's eyes followed the bend of her ankle, the shapely arch of her foot. "Sure," she replied. "I shouldn't be doing this, you know. I never socialize with the clients."

"It's a big pool. No point in letting it go to waste."

"No, there's not." Suddenly she cast him an impish grin and got to her feet. "Race?"

Cassie was in the water with a graceful jackknife of slender limbs almost before Shane knew what she was about. She was two lengths ahead and a surprisingly strong swimmer, but Shane had the advantage of height and years of muscles conditioned by hard work. Still, he had to use effort to outdistance her, and was glad when, at the end of the third lap, she braced herself against the side of the pool and gasped, "Okay! Your match!"

He felt absurdly gratified as he turned in the water and balanced himself on the top step, grinning and breathing hard. Generally he didn't like women who competed with him on any level—especially when they came close to winning—but the race had actually been fun. "You're a good swimmer," he told her.

"All-state champion in high school," she replied, her voice a little choppy with exertion and the laughter of exhilaration.

He liked the way she looked with her hair slicked back and her eyes washed a brilliant green by chlorine and sunshine. She smoothed the water away from her face with both hands and, in an unexpected motion, suddenly brought them down flat against the surface of the water, splashing him.

She laughed at his startled exclamation and started to swim away, but he caught her by the arm and a playful water fight ensued. Shane went under more than once and so did she, and when she grasped his shoulders and tried to unbalance him by wrapping a leg around his ankle, he suddenly reversed the positions, catching her under the arms and pinning her close with her leg trapped between both of his.

Their laughter faded into a sort of pleased recognition of the closeness. Shane was aware of the pressure of her fingers on his bare shoulders, the suppleness of her muscles, the curve of her small breasts just above his thumbs. And there was a light in her eyes that revealed she enjoyed the touch as much as he did.

"You don't play fair," she said.

He could see her chest rise and fall beneath the water, could feel the rapid rhythm of her heart beneath the curve of his hand, which was, he knew, only from exercise. He slid his hands down to her waist. "Neither do you."

She lowered her eyes and moved her hands to his chest, exerting a small pressure. He let her go, and watched the water cascade off her body as she climbed out of the pool.

She walked across the deck, found a stack of towels and dried her face before spreading the towel on a chair. "That was nice," she said breathlessly. She picked up her bottle of beer and drank. "I can't remember when I've had so much exercise in such a short time."

Shane lifted himself out of the pool and reached for his own towel. "That beer's probably warm. Do you want another one?"

"No thanks." She set the almost-empty bottle back on the deck and stretched out on the chaise. "I don't really drink beer."

Shane grinned and uncapped another one for her. He lay back in the chaise next to hers, and for a time they shared the sun in companionable silence. Occasionally Cassie would sip from her bottle, and more than occasionally Shane would let his eyes stray to the shape of her legs or the curve of her hip or the tiny beads of water that were evaporating from her chest. This, he realized slowly, was what he had always pictured when he thought about being married: being comfortable with someone, talking when it was good to talk and being silent when it was not; playing and laughing and relaxing together; admiring the way the sun shone on her hair or the way she curved her wrist when she lifted the bottle to drink...just enjoying being with her.

The fact that it was Cassie Averil who made him feel that way was a little disconcerting, and he wasn't sure it made sense. Nor was he sure he wanted to think about it.

After a time he thought it might be better to talk, so he said, "How'd you get into this matchmaking business, anyway?"

Cassie smiled behind her dark glasses. "It's a long story. My grandmother did it, then my mother. Most of those wedding pictures on the walls belong to them. I majored in psychology and was interested in human behavior. Still, I never seriously considered a dating service as a career. But it was a funny thing." Her expression grew thoughtful as she took another sip from the bottle. "For college graduation my parents gave me a trip to Hawaii. I was lying on the beach—

you know how crowded the beach is at Waikiki." She glanced at him.

"Never been."

"Oh? Well, you should. It's wonderful. Anyway, I was lying there soaking up the sun, the way I'm doing now, and there was this couple next to me. As I said, the beach was crowded and I couldn't help overhearing them. At first I thought they had just met—maybe a pickup on the beach or something, because they sounded so silly and awkward with each other, you know. He was asking her if she liked seafood and she was asking him if he liked to read and it was apparent they didn't know each other at all. The longer I listened, the more I expected one of them to just say 'So long. It was nice to meet you,' because it was obvious they had nothing in common and the silence got longer and longer as they tried to find something to talk about. Then I happened to glance over. Well, I didn't 'just happen,'" she confessed. "I was curious, and I noticed they were wearing matching wedding bands that were so new the shine wasn't even dull yet. Those two were on their honeymoon and were just then discovering they had married strangers!"

She paused and took another sip of the beer. "It was at that moment that I knew what I wanted my life's work to be. If those two had come to me first, they never would have ended up on a beach in Waikiki trying to think of something to say to each other for the rest of their lives."

"But they *did* get married," Shane pointed out. "They must have had some reason."

"Sure. They fell in love, and in that mad rush of passion they decided marriage sounded like a good idea. People are such fools."

Shane couldn't prevent an indulgent twitch of his lips. "And you, of course, know better."

"Of course, that's my profession. Not only do I know what ingredients to look for in the making of a relationship, but I can be objective and see things the people involved chose to overlook. That's why people in the old days used to arrange marriages for their children, you know, because most people don't know what's good for them in a situation like that. I'll tell you something," she added, drinking again. "The world would be a lot better off if all marriages were still arranged. Those marriages lasted a lifetime."

"Yeah, but the average life span back then was only twenty-nine years."

She shrugged. "A lifetime is a lifetime."

"I've seen pictures of some of those poker-faced women from the castle-and-dungeon days," Shane said thoughtfully. "I guess if I had to spend my life married to one of them, I wouldn't want to live past twenty-nine, either."

Cassie grinned and shook her head.

"What about you, Cassie?" Shane asked seriously after a moment. "Don't you ever think about making a match for yourself? Having a family?"

Generally Cassie would have ignored a question like that, or tactfully steered the conversation in another direction. It might have been the beer, or the sun and the relaxed atmosphere of the pool, but her usual reserve seemed to be melting away. She seemed to have no trouble talking to Shane—even about that.

"Oh, I don't know," she answered thoughtfully, twirling the beer bottle slowly between her palms. "I guess I've thought about it, but not very seriously. Marriage, a family—they just never seemed right for me. Maybe I'm just one of those people who was meant to have a career and nothing else."

"Sounds kind of sad to me."

"Not really. I like my life." She might have sounded just a touch too defensive, so she added lightly, "Besides, my standards are impossibly high. I could never find a match for myself."

Shane lifted his beer to her in a gentle salute. "A loss to men everywhere."

"You'd better believe it."

Shane chuckled as she finished off her beer and set the empty bottle on the deck with a flourish. She smiled at him, aware that she hadn't felt so comfortable with anyone in a long time. "You know," she said, "the first day you came into the office, I thought you were a real jerk."

"I know."

"I just wanted to apologize for that." It suddenly seemed very important that he understand, and her tone grew earnest as she explained, "It's just that— well, there aren't many men like you around, and I guess I had trouble believing you were real. But you're open and sincere and all you really want to do is commit to someone and raise a family. That *is* rare, Shane. And I meant what I said before—any woman would be lucky to have you."

His expression softened in a way that made Cassie's cheeks tingle unexpectedly, and he said gently, "That's nice, coming from you. It really is."

They shared a tenuous moment that seemed to come from nowhere, hovering on the edge of revelation yet drawing back shyly before the first word was spoken. And though Cassie felt she should say more, and wanted to hear more, confusion made it impossible. She knew it was best.

Then Shane moved suddenly, reaching beneath his chair to bring up a bottle of sunscreen lotion. "You'd better use some of this," he said lightly, tossing it to her. "You're going to burn."

Shane tried not to watch as she began to spread the lotion over her legs and arms, then he felt silly for making himself look away. Since when had it been illegal to look at a pretty girl in a swimsuit? It was simply that their relationship was a nebulous one and he wasn't sure what boundaries it encompassed. Was there something immoral about a man being attracted to his matchmaker?

He decided there probably was, but that didn't stop him from looking. He watched her spread lotion over her shoulders and her chest and noticed a small spattering of freckles beneath her collarbone that he found endearing. "How'd you ever get a name like Cassie?" he asked.

She glanced at him, amused. "How'd you ever get a name like Shane?"

He shrugged. "I guess that's something we'll never know. There's no one to ask."

Cassie was a little embarrassed for having forgotten that fact, and she recapped the bottle of sunscreen without looking at him. "Cassie's short for Cassandra. She was a prophetess from classical literature."

He nodded. "Just like you."

"I beg your pardon?"

"Didn't you tell me you know things about me nobody else knows—even me?"

She laughed and stretched out in the chaise. "That's not prophecy. That's psychology."

"Well?" He got up and went to the cooler. "When are you going to tell me about myself?"

Cassie watched him speculatively, then came to a decision. "Okay. For one thing, you're not really the kind of man who can be happy doing nothing for very long. You've been active all your life and you're not ready to retire. In less than six months you'll be going out of your mind looking for something to do."

He chuckled as he lifted a beer from the ice. "Watch me prove you wrong. Do you want a Coke or something?"

"Actually, I was just getting used to the taste of the beer."

He uncapped two beers and brought one over to her. "Go ahead," he invited.

"All right." She sipped the beer thoughtfully. "You're ambitious, determined and just a little bit reckless. You're also a lot smarter than you pretend."

He grinned and leaned back in his chair. "You must have me mixed up with somebody else. I'm the laziest man I know, and there's not a reckless bone in my body. Ask Jack. He's been trying to get me to go to

Vegas for three weekends in a row. As for smart, well, I barely finished high school."

"A lazy man couldn't have turned a laborer's salary into a fortune in fifteen years," Cassie pointed out. "You didn't just stumble into success, Shane Bartlett, you planned it. You took risks, you thought it through, you made it happen. And you'll do it again if you have to." She drank from the bottle again. "Believe me, I've been around oil men all my life. There's a certain chemistry about the good ones—a kind of combination of shrewdness and talent that sets them apart from ordinary people and lets you know there's no stopping them. You're that kind of man."

Shane merely grinned and shook his head.

"You're adventurous, unorthodox and experimentative," she went on. "You like to be challenged. You even like conflict to a certain degree. If you had lived a century earlier, you might have been a cowboy or an Indian fighter or a merchant sailor—"

"Too much work."

"You're impulsive and contrary. All it takes is for somebody to tell you a thing can't be done and you'll dig your heels in and do it—your way. Telling me to find you a wife inside a month is a perfect example of that. And any man who holds on to a pair of boots that should have been thrown out with the trash ten years ago has got to be just a little bit sentimental."

"Those are my lucky boots," he objected.

Her eyes twinkled as she glanced at him. "Add superstitious to the list."

"This is crazy."

"And for these and other reasons," Cassie concluded blithely, "I couldn't possibly match you up with the kind of woman you first described to me. You'd be bored out of your head. If you don't know yourself, you can't possibly know what you want."

Shane frowned. "Do you mean to tell me this Melinda Hollander—"

"Mindy," Cassie corrected. "Mindy Howard."

"Whatever. She's going to turn out to be some kind of intellectual know-it-all who reads the financial page and jumps out of airplanes for kicks, right?"

Cassie chuckled. "Nothing like that at all. I told you, she's a nice girl and you have a lot in common. She just has a little more depth than you'd suspect. Just like you do. Which means you'll have a lot more in common."

Shane looked uncomfortable. "I've got to tell you that I'm not easy in my mind about any of this."

"Relax," she assured him. "That's what you have me for."

Cassie only wished she felt as secure in her decision as she sounded. Not that she had any doubts about Mindy; she *was* perfect for Shane, and Cassie had every confidence that the potential existed for a genuine relationship between them. It was just that—perhaps that was the problem. Maybe she had done her job too well. And as much as it shamed her to admit it, there was a part of her that wished Mindy hadn't been so available and so easy to find, that wished she could have had more time to introduce Shane to some not-quite-so-perfect women, that even, unlikely as it was, almost hoped something unpredictable would happen and Mindy and Shane wouldn't get along as well as she knew they would. It was incomprehensible, it was unforgivable, and Cassie couldn't believe she was actually feeling that way. But after Shane met Mindy there would be no more Sunday afternoons by the pool for her, no more bantering conversations with a man who grew more interesting each time she met him, no more warm brown eyes and quick smiles. And that made her sorry. Cassie was ashamed of herself, but just this one time she wished she hadn't been quite so good at her job.

She glanced over at Shane, and it was the oddest thing—for a brief moment, as her eyes met his, it was almost as though he knew what she was thinking. His expression was thoughtful, touched with a shade of regret, and Cassie felt a stab of yearning that surprised and embarrassed her. Quickly she looked away and took another sip of her beer.

The sun grew higher, and they talked in a desultory fashion, sometimes about her, sometimes about him. A lethargy stole over Cassie that made the day seem timeless. She couldn't remember when she had been so relaxed, nor when she had known a man who was so easy to be with. She forgot about Mindy, she forgot about work, and she simply enjoyed Shane.

When the puppy woke up, Cassie turned over onto her stomach and rolled a tennis ball back and forth for him, laughing lazily at the puppy's efforts to catch it. After a while Shane got up and joined the game, retrieving the ball when the puppy missed and rolling it back to Cassie. It was a silly way to spend the afternoon, but maybe that was one of the secrets to life: having the grace to just be silly every now and then.

When the puppy grew bored and wandered off to explore the courtyard, Cassie closed her eyes drowsily. She opened them again with a start when she felt Shane's hands on her bare shoulder blades.

"You need some sunscreen on your back," he said, and held up the bottle. "Do you mind?"

"Oh..." She tried to make her voice sound casual as she shifted over to make room for him beside her on the chaise. "Thank you."

But her heart was beating hard as he sat next to her, his bare thigh touching her hip. His hands spread the lotion in a gliding, circular motion over her shoulders and the middle of her back, sliding toward the low dip of her swimsuit at the base of her spine.

"Am I making you nervous?"

"No." Her voice was muffled in her arms, which she hoped would disguise the lie. "Why?"

"Your muscles are tense."

"Oh. I guess I'm just not used to this." If only he knew how long it had been since she had felt a man's touch. How strange it was, and how wonderful.

He started to recap the bottle. "I'll stop."

"No," she said quickly. And it was difficult to keep her tone offhand as she added, "Not unless you want to. It feels kind of nice."

She was glad she couldn't see his expression as he poured more lotion into his hand and finished spreading it on her lower back.

Cassie closed her eyes as his hands played a soothing rhythm over her sun-drenched skin, penetrating her muscles and stroking her nerves into a new and singular awareness. It was sensual and it was natural; it was arousing yet relaxing; it was perfectly innocent . . . and it wasn't.

She could feel his shadow moving over her, shielding her from the sun in patches and waves, and his heat against her side. The air smelled of coconut oil and sunshine and that clean, indefinable fragrance that was Shane. She had never felt so aware, yet so paradoxically lethargic, as though his nearness were a drug that both enhanced the senses and muted the will.

When his hand moved from her back to her thigh, her pulse quickened and the nerve cells of her skin seemed to flare, but still she didn't object. He spread the lotion in a single, slow, caressing stroke from the curve of her buttock to the crease of her knee, and every sense she possessed was concentrated on his hands as he encircled her thigh and applied the slippery lotion down and around, shaping her muscles with his fingertips. He caressed her calf and her ankle. He took her foot in both hands and massaged it gently. Cassie's breath quickened and her toes curled. Then he gave the same slow, thorough attention to the other leg.

Cassie's stomach muscles tightened as his hands massaged her knee and began a lingering, upward caress, his fingertips just brushing the apex of her thighs. Her breath caught and there was a lightness, almost a dizziness, in her chest as sensations almost forgotten fluttered to life within her. All the world seemed to pause before his next move, his next breath.

His hands moved over her hips and lightly cupped her waist. She could feel him bending over her, very close, could hear the slightly increased rhythm of his breathing. "Cassie?" he asked softly.

She turned over. Her hazy vision was filled with the gentleness of his face, the drowsy heat in his eyes. His bare chest brushed her breasts, and she thought he could feel the furious thumping of her heart.

She lifted an unsteady hand to his face and he turned to her caress, brushing her fingertips with a kiss. Slowly, and with great absorption, her fingers moved down over his throat to his collarbone, across his chest, tangling lightly in the damp hair there. She opened her palm against the taut muscle of his breast, and she could feel his heart beat.

His fingertips lightly stroked the back of her wrist. He said nothing, but there was alertness in his eyes, cautiously mixed with question. And there was desire in his eyes and in hers, and only the slightest motion, the merest breath, would make that desire a fact...and Cassie held her breath. This was wrong and shouldn't be happening, and she was the one who had to stop it.

But for the longest moment her eyes were caught by his. Her breath wouldn't leave her chest, and she didn't know whether she could make herself do what she had to do. Then, somehow, her hand tightened against his chest, pushing a little, and her voice sounded hoarse and very far away as she said deliberately, "I have to go now."

He lowered his eyes and let his fingertips trail down her arm as she dropped her hand. After what seemed like a very long time, he moved away.

Cassie swung her feet to the deck and sat up. She felt dizzy and disoriented. Sitting there for a moment, she frowned with concentration as she tried to get her bearings. Her skin still tingled with his touch and her heart was beating sluggishly. Yet it seemed at the same time as though what had just happened—or had almost happened—was a pleasant and faraway dream, something she treasured but for which she wasn't responsible.

Shane retrieved her sandals, and she smiled at him uncertainly. Her fingers were clumsy and she couldn't manage the straps, so Shane fastened them for her. She smiled at him again. "Well," she said. How strange her voice sounded! "Thanks for a pleasant afternoon."

She grasped the hand he offered her and pulled herself up, then somehow lost her balance and stumbled against him. He caught her under the arms and chuckled softly. "Darlin', you're not going anywhere."

She pushed at her sunglasses and held on to his arm to steady herself. "No, it's late and I—"

"You're in no condition to drive."

"Don't be silly." She tried to be insulted but couldn't quite manage it. "I only had two beers—"

"Four, but who's counting?" His eyes twinkled with a mixture of indulgence and sympathy. "And I'll bet you didn't have anything to eat before you came over here, did you?"

She hesitated. "I don't think so. I don't remember."

He nodded and slipped an arm around her waist. "Too much sun and too much beer on an empty stomach will do it to you every time. Come on inside and lie down for a while. You'll feel better after a nap."

She felt she should protest, but couldn't concentrate long enough to do so. Besides, it felt good to walk with Shane's arm around her waist and her head on his shoulder. To protest anything at that moment would have been foolish.

Her overheated skin prickled in the air-conditioned trailer, and she shivered. Shane guided her to the bed and pulled back the covers.

"I'll get suntan lotion all over your bed," she objected.

"That's okay." He smiled as he took her shoulders and gently pressed her to sit on the edge of the bed. "I like the smell."

He slipped off her sandals and swung her legs over the side of the bed. Cassie took off her sunglasses, dropped them onto the floor, then sank down into the cool pillows, drifting contentedly, carefree. "This is nice," she murmured. "You're nice."

He moved to draw the covers over her, and his eyes were so warm, his smile so tender, that it seemed the most natural thing in the world for Cassie to loop her arms around his neck and kiss him.

The only thing she could think of was drowning—suffused by sweetness, soft, rushing, liquid heat, inundated with his taste, his scent, melting into him. She opened her mouth and his tongue entered, her fingers drifted through his hair, her breasts pressed upward into the hard musculature of his chest. His hand slipped beneath her back, strong fingers on bare skin, pressing her upward, and she felt his indrawn breath as she cupped his face and turned slightly to taste him more thoroughly, drinking of him, insatiable.

Her eyelids fluttered when his lips left hers, but she couldn't quite open them. Her body seemed to be throbbing with a million separate heartbeats, distant yet aware, aching yet content. His lips brushed her cheek, and it was an exquisitely beautiful sensation that seemed to last forever. She tried to lift her hand to his face, but her limbs were watery and uncoordinated. Still, even that didn't matter. She wanted to lie there for the rest of her life and revel in the sensation that he created with his touch.

"Shane . . ." she murmured.

"Yes." His voice was soft, almost a whisper. "I know."

"I don't want you to leave."

"Don't worry. I won't."

The last thing Cassie was aware of was his fingers stroking her cheek before she drifted off into the soft cloud of sleep.

It was dark inside the trailer when Cassie awoke. At first she was startled and disoriented, but too soon the memories came flooding back. Cassie flung back the covers and swung her feet to the floor, doubling over to muffle a soft moan of sheer humiliation.

She wanted to tell herself that intoxication had loosened her inhibitions and made her do things she would never ordinarily do. It would have been very easy to tell herself that; she would still be embarrassed, but at least she wouldn't be responsible. The truth was that she had known exactly what she was doing, and the only thing that had been affected by the alcohol was her good judgment. And her humiliation wasn't so much over her behavior but the fact that she had fallen asleep when she had—and that Shane was probably laughing to himself over what a sloppy drunk she made.

She fumbled for the lamp switch on the bedside table and found her shoes and sunglasses on the floor. She exchanged the sunglasses for regular glasses from her purse, then went quickly into the bathroom to change her clothes.

The first thing she noticed when she stepped hesitantly out into the twilight was the smell of charcoal in the air. The second thing she noticed was a string of citronella candles suspended from a wire that ran from a nearby tree limb to the edge of the trailer. They looked like dancing fireflies in the dying light.

Shane had set up a grill in front of the trailer. He was turning a steak that was almost the size of the grill top. Then he noticed her and smiled. Cassie felt her whole body go scarlet with embarrassment, and she didn't know how to begin to apologize or explain. She could hardly meet his eyes and was grateful for the dusk that hid her misery.

And just when she thought she would wither away from awkwardness, Shane put the barbecue fork down and said easily, "Just look at that sky, will you? I tell you, no place on earth has got Texas beat for sunsets."

Cassie released a grateful breath, and she thought that if it were possible to fall in love with a man in a single moment, that would have been the moment and he would have been the man.

She turned her gaze to the sky and let the deep indigo and pale pink swirls soothe her jagged nerves and wash away the edges of tension. "It is beautiful," she said softly. "No matter how often I see it, I'm always amazed at how big the Texas sky is. A person could get lost just looking at it.''

He came over and gestured her to sit on the steps. When she did, he sat beside her, and even after everything that had happened the silence was comfortable between them.

''I like the candles, too,'' she said. ''But you do know that they make electronic bug repellers, don't you?''

''I know. But I like the way the candles look. More romantic somehow.''

''There's nothing romantic about the sound of a moth hitting two hundred and fifty volts of electricity,'' she agreed, and he laughed softly. Cassie tightened her hands around her knee and knew the moment had come. ''I guess,'' she said without looking at him, ''I made a pretty big fool of myself this afternoon.''

''Did you?''

She nodded.

Though she still couldn't make herself look at him, she could feel his eyes on her intently. ''Does that mean you're sorry?''

Her throat tightened. She didn't want to answer that, but she had to. She focused on her fingers, which were pressed into the fabric of her skirt that covered her knees. ''Only,'' she managed with difficulty, ''if you think I . . . come on to every man like that, or . . . that it was just the beer and the sun.''

Something seemed to quicken in the air around them, and she could hear the alertness in his voice as he answered softly, ''I don't think that, Cassie.''

She looked at him in a rush of relief that was swiftly followed by tenderness. His face was gently shadowed in the dying light and highlighted by the glow of the candles overhead. She wanted to loosen her fingers and let them travel the planes of that face, to say at least one of the things that were aching inside her. But she kept her fingers tightly clasped and only said, "Good. Because I wouldn't want you to think—"

"I wouldn't. It was my fault, anyway. I shouldn't—"

"No, it wasn't. I just—"

"I know you're not the kind of woman who would—"

"Good," she said again. And after the rush of half-formed conversation the silence that fell was thick with expectation. He held her eyes for a minute, then looked away. Cassie dropped her gaze to her knees. She could feel her heart beating. There was more she wanted to say and more he wanted to say, but neither one of them dared to speak first. And it was better that way. Both of them knew that.

"I have to go home now," Cassie said abruptly, and got to her feet.

"You can't go without dinner," Shane objected, rising as well. "How am I supposed to live with myself, sending you home on an empty stomach?"

Cassie smiled. "Thanks, but I'm still feeling a little queasy. I'd better not."

He glanced toward the grill. "Look at the size of that steak. Are you going to make me eat it all by myself?"

She laughed. "I'm sure you won't have any trouble."

His smile told her he wouldn't insist, but there was still a gentle persuasion in his eyes. "You sure you won't stay? That's a hell of a sirloin I've got going, if I do say so myself."

Cassie hesitated. Dinner with Shane under a canopy of stars and a circle of candles... "Thanks," she said, "but I've got a long drive and I don't want to be on the road too long after dark."

"I can take you home."

Yes, he could take her home...tonight, or in the morning. She swallowed. "I need my car." If he had asked her to stay one more time, she might have done it. But he didn't, and she didn't give him much time to try again. "I've had a nice time, Shane. I wish..."

But she stopped, uncertain how she wanted to finish that sentence. She wished the day didn't have to end. She wished she could stay. She wished he would insist she stay. She wished everything could be different....

He was looking at her intently, and there was an insistent undertone in his voice as he prompted softly, "What? What do you wish, Cassie?"

Cassie dropped her eyes. "I don't know. Nothing. Good night."

She started to turn away, but he caught her hand. "Cassie."

She turned back quickly. "Yes?"

She couldn't tell in the dim light what his expression was. He looked at her for a moment as if he wanted to say something, and then he smiled and dropped her hand. "Nothing. Drive carefully, okay?"

Her smile was a little weak. "Okay."

She walked to her car and drove away, and Shane watched until the taillights of her car disappeared from view. He had dinner alone and ended up feeding most of the steak to the dog.

Seven

Shane's date with Mindy Howard was arranged for Wednesday night. Generally Cassie would have handled the details herself, especially with a case as important as this one, but she no longer trusted herself to be involved in anything that concerned Shane Bartlett. So she turned the case over to Emma and tried, largely unsuccessfully, to give her attention to others who needed it.

On Wednesday the anxiety built inside her like a hot spring straining to crack the surface of the earth. She chewed two pencils, she broke a fingernail tapping on her desk, she put her hand on the telephone three times to call Shane. But what would she say to him? Have a good time? Let me know what happens? Don't go?

At 5:45 she went out into the reception area. "Did you tell Shane that daisies are Mindy's favorite?" she asked Emma.

"I certainly did." Emma was unpacking the contents of her purse, apparently looking for something.

"Did you order some sent to her in case he forgets?"

Emma pulled out a pair of driving shoes, a pair of house slippers and a bundle of crocheting. "All taken care of."

"And you're going to meet them at the restaurant and make the introductions?"

"At seven o'clock." Emma fished out a paperback book, looked at it quizzically, then added it to the pile. "I'll be out of there by 7:05."

"Actually," Cassie said hesitantly, "you could stay and have a drink if you want. Just to make sure things are going smoothly."

"Nonsense. You've always said our most important asset was to know when to make ourselves scarce. Besides, I have a bridge game tonight, and I'll be late as it is."

That was Cassie's cue to volunteer to go in Emma's place, and any other time she would have. But in this case she didn't dare.

Emma extracted a hairpin with a triumphant expression and used it to fasten one loose curl behind her ear. "I do declare, Cassie. I've never seen you so jumpy. You'd think I'd never done this before. Everything's under control. I promise you."

"No, it's not that," Cassie assured her. "It's just that you know how important this case is and I want everything to be perfect."

"Well, we've done the best we can and the rest is up to them."

Emma began to repack her purse. "You know," she added, "that Mr. Bartlett is a nice young man. It's a pity."

Cassie had started to wander restlessly back to her office. Now she turned. "What is?"

Emma seemed to debate over a half-finished roll of candy, then put it back into her purse. "That he has to go to some other girl. You should have snatched him up when you had the chance."

A flush of guilt started in Cassie's chest and went all the way up to her forehead. "Don't be silly. I never date clients. It's unethical."

"Not really," Emma pointed out, struggling with the clasp on her purse. "The man came in here looking for the perfect match, and if it happens to be you..."

"Me!" Defensiveness made Cassie's laugh a little shrill. "Believe me, no one could be further from Shane Bartlett's perfect match than me—and vice versa."

"He's awfully good-looking."

"Well, sure. I mean, if you like that type." Unconsciously Cassie twisted her fingers together as she paced toward the window. "I mean, I won't deny he has a certain sex appeal. But if all I wanted was someone to... to have a fling with, I certainly wouldn't have to look at my own client list for that, would I?" She turned to Emma a little anxiously.

"I suppose not." Emma got her purse fastened, then glanced in dismay at the paperback book still lying on her desk. She began to unpack her purse again. "All I know is that it's a shame a pretty girl like you is still single at your age. And when I think of all those years working with your mother, and now you, matching other people up, it just doesn't seem right somehow that the one person who never made a match was you."

Cassie grinned, relaxing a little. "And you," she pointed out.

"Oh, pshaw! I'm an old woman. I'm not interested in things like that."

But Cassie thought she saw a faint flush of pink stain Emma's cheeks, and her curiosity was aroused. Before she could pursue that, however, Emma went on, "It just seems to me that a smart girl like you would have sense enough to give a man like Shane Bartlett a second look the next time one walks into the office."

"Just because a man looks good doesn't mean he's good for me," Cassie replied, and the exasperation in her voice was only an exaggerated denial. "I mean, for heaven's sake, I'm everything he *doesn't* want in a woman, and once you get past that surface charm of his, there's absolutely nothing to appeal to a woman like me. Sure, he's nice enough. You might even say very nice...tender, and thoughtful, and even sensitive in a way...."

She was aware of a slight wistfulness in her tone and quickly toughened it. "But you don't build a relationship on niceness. Lots of people are nice. You've got to have common interests, similar goals and needs, and Shane Bartlett and I are at exact opposite ends of the spectrum. I mean, to even consider a man like him for myself would violate every principle I believe in. It would negate all the years of research I've built the business around and it would just be downright silly. Wouldn't it?''

Emma had stopped rummaging in her purse and was looking at Cassie with an alert interest. Cassie realized that she had sounded like a lady who protests too much, and tried to cover it with a quick laugh and a lift of her shoulders.

''Well, it's all hypothetical, anyway,'' Cassie said, ''since I've already found Shane Bartlett's perfect match and—'' She glanced at her watch and tried to disguise the sinking feeling she felt in her stomach. ''He's probably leaving right about now to pick her up. So—'' she released a breath and painted on a smile that she was certain looked as false as it felt ''—I guess there's no reason for me to hang around here, either.''

''That's right, dear, you go on home.'' Emma turned back to her purse. ''Make yourself a nice dinner and go to bed early. You've been wound up like a top all week. You could use the rest.''

''Yes,'' Cassie agreed, and squared her shoulders determinedly. The sooner she got out of the office, the sooner she could stop thinking about Shane. ''That's just what I'll do. After all, it's out of our hands now, isn't it?''

''Don't worry. I'm sure everything will be just fine. After all, they're perfect for each other, aren't they?''

Some of Cassie's resolve faded, and her shoulders began to sag. ''Yes,'' she said weakly. ''I suppose they are.''

And it was too late to do anything about it now, anyway.

By eight o'clock Cassie had eaten dinner, fed the cat and washed her hair. She pulled on a nightshirt and a madras wrap robe and roamed around the apartment trying not to think about Shane. *It's going to be fine,* she kept telling herself. *Mindy's going to adore Shane and he's going to see in her the perfect little wife and they're going to be very happy together.* Cassie knew her job. Mindy and Shane were meant for each other. She had nothing to worry about. Then why was she so unhappy?

She turned on the television and tried to watch a few minutes of a situation comedy but couldn't concentrate. It was 8:10. They were probably through the first course by now. Shane was telling amusing stories and Mindy's eyes were sparkling. Mindy had a great figure and she knew how to show it off. Shane's eyes would be dropping to her cleavage every now and then just as they had done with Cassie, and Mindy would pretend not to notice but would be preening inside, just as Cassie had done.

"Damn it all anyway!" Cassie muttered, and flipped off the television set with a vicious gesture.

She went into the kitchen, poured herself a diet soda and sat down at the kitchen table to drink it. She didn't know what she was so upset about. She should be proud of herself. On a short deadline she had made a match that she had every reason to believe was perfect. If this worked out the way she was certain it would, her theories would be vindicated under the most challenging of circumstances. And there was no reason in the world it shouldn't work out.

Shane would be a loyal and devoted husband. Mindy would...

Mindy didn't deserve him, Cassie decided abruptly. What could a twenty-three-year-old know about keeping a man like Shane happy? How could she possibly appreciate the depth, the thoughtfulness, the lonely little boy that was hidden behind Shane's carefree facade? How could she see the value of a sunset or the sweetness of a silence? How could a woman like Mindy Howard know anything at all about *life*?

"Stop it," Cassie commanded herself, and took a long, cooling drink of the soda. She was being ridiculous. She was inventing excuses and there was no reason for it. Everything was going to work out fine.

For a while she tried to divert herself by planning how she would spend the rest of Shane's fee. Somehow that wasn't as much fun as it once would have been.

At 8:45 she looked at her watch. They would be approaching dessert now. She smiled a little as she remembered how Shane loved desserts. But the smile faded when she remembered that Mindy had listed "baking" as one of her favorite indoor pastimes.

Cassie wandered back to the living room and thought about calling Emma, just to get her impression of the meeting. But what could Emma tell her after five minutes of seeing the two of them together? Besides, Emma had said she was playing bridge tonight and Cassie didn't want to interrupt.

She picked up a book and tried to read. It was nine-thirty when she looked at her watch again. She wondered what Shane had planned after dinner. Maybe he would just take Mindy home. That would be the proper thing to do on a first date.

She wondered if he would kiss her good-night. She wondered if he would stay the night.

She tossed the book aside and lay back on the sofa, staring morosely at the ceiling, wondering a lot of things.

A month ago, if a woman like Mindy Howard had walked into his life, Shane would have thought his dreams had come true. She had smooth blond hair that reached to her shoulders and was brushed behind her ears in a simple, casual style. Her eyes were blue. She had a cute pixie face that was appealing but not at all glamorous, and he liked her laugh. She didn't wear too much makeup or jewelry. She seemed a little shy at first, which he had always taken for a good sign in a woman.

But as they sat down to dinner he thought the color of her hair seemed a little too bright and was probably dyed. She had lovely breasts, round and high, and a tiny waist, but he thought her dress was too tight and cut too low. She certainly knew how to keep a man entertained, asking questions that encouraged him to talk about himself, but after a while Shane saw through the ploy and found it boring. She had almost nothing to say about herself.

It did turn out that she liked camping and fishing, but confessed she wasn't much of an athlete. Shane wondered if she would go to fat in a few years. Her father had died when she was young and she had raised three brothers and sisters while her mother worked. She confessed that the only thing she had ever considered herself to be really good at was raising children and keeping house. Shane asked her if she had any other interests, and she couldn't think of one.

She explained that she had joined the dating service because she was new in town and it was hard for her to meet people. Shane agreed that the same thing was true for him. By that time he had told his life story and she had told all he wanted to hear of hers, and conversation lagged.

He tried to figure out why he wasn't tripping all over himself to make an impression on this girl. Anyone could see she was perfect for him. A man could spend hours just watching the changing expressions in those navy blue eyes—if he weren't so busy remembering snapping green ones instead. She was sexy—no denying that. She loved to cook, she was crazy about children, she confessed she had seen all of the world she wanted to see and was ready to settle down. She professed the same enthusiasm for chocolate torte and college football that he did, and she even did needlepoint, for heaven's sake. And how could any man be bored with a woman who hung on his every word and made him feel as though there was nothing else in the world of any consequence except him?

But Shane was bored. And he began to wonder uneasily whether Cassie was right. Maybe he didn't know what he wanted.

Because all he could think of the whole time he was with Mindy was the way Cassie's locket had gleamed against the dip between her breasts in the candlelight. And the way Cassie had of slanting her eyes at him in disapproval, and how she could make his temper flare with her dry words. He missed her quick wit and honeyed drawl. The scent of lemon and vanilla haunted the back of his mind. And auburn hair was, after all, much more attractive than blond.

Mindy and Shane had arrived in separate cars, and he was glad he didn't have to take her home. He told her what a pleasure it was meeting her, and she seemed disappointed when he didn't say anything about calling her again. He didn't kiss her good night, nor even think about it. Later, he supposed she might have been insulted by that.

It was barely ten o'clock and the evening seemed to have lasted forever. He couldn't blame Cassie for that. She had done her job and had delivered what she had promised. The only trouble was, what she had promised wasn't what he needed at all.

There was a peculiar kind of tightness in his chest and his mind was crowded as Shane got into his car and started for home. Nothing made sense anymore, and it should have been so simple. All he had ever wanted was a sweet, quiet woman capable of returning his love and being his wife. Mindy Howard had shown every possibility of being that woman. Then what was wrong with him? Why couldn't he just relax and let it happen? What more did he want, anyway?

He thought he knew the answer to that when, twenty minutes later, he found himself not on the highway leading out of town, but parked in front of Cassie Averil's apartment building.

When the doorbell rang Cassie thought it might be Emma and she rushed to answer it. Emma must have known how anxious Cassie was and had stopped by after her bridge game to report on how the meeting had gone. She tripped over Fluffy in her hurry to open the door and received a loud yowl in reprimand. Flinging open the door, she simply stared in astonishment when she saw Shane standing there.

"Hi," he said. His eyes swept over her cotton robe, her towel-dried hair and her bare feet and he added, "Is it too late to be stopping by? Should I have called first?"

"I, uh, no." Cassie self-consciously pulled the lapels of her robe together and pushed back her hair. "I'm just—I didn't expect to see you."

"Hello there, Fluffy." Shane bent down and scooped up the cat as she tried to wind between his feet. "I just thought you might like to hear how it went tonight. Do you mind if I come in?"

"No." Cassie quickly stepped away from the door. "Please do."

He stepped inside, still holding the cat, and Cassie gestured him toward the sofa. "Would you like something to drink or anything?"

"I'm fine thanks." He sat down, and Fluffy posed with her forepaws on his jacket, begging for her ears to be scratched. Shane obliged.

Cassie wasn't sure whether she felt relief or trepidation as she glanced at her watch. "It's not even ten-thirty," she said. "Wasn't that a short evening?"

He shrugged, drawing his hand down Fluffy's back. "Long enough for me."

Cassie looked at him sharply. "What do you mean? What went wrong? What did you do?"

"What makes you think *I* did something?" he retorted. "Why couldn't it have been her? Or even you?"

"Me? I wasn't even there!"

"You fixed us up, didn't you?"

"She was perfect for you!"

"Yeah. Perfectly boring."

Cassie did a half turn on the carpet, thrusting her fingers through her hair. Her heart was beating fast, and the adrenaline that surged through her was partly dismay and partly exhilaration. Shane hadn't liked her! All those things she had spent the evening tormenting herself over hadn't happened. *Nothing* had happened. Why hadn't it occurred to her that Shane might not like her?

And then there was the dismay. She had failed. She had done her best. She had matched him with the perfect mate—and he didn't like her. That meant there was something desperately wrong with her methods, that she didn't know what she was doing, that she had made a promise she couldn't keep, that she had a contract she couldn't fulfill.

She turned on him, her eyes narrowing. "You're doing this deliberately, aren't you? You never believed the girl I chose for you would be the right one. You never wanted to cooperate from the beginning. You wouldn't even fill out the form! You've sabotaged this whole thing!''

"Why would I do a thing like that?" Shane got up, bringing the cat with him. He couldn't believe he was raising his voice at her when he had come here to... He was no longer sure what he had come here for. He only knew that the sparks in her eyes and the color in her cheeks sent a surge of excitement through him. He'd felt more alive in the past three minutes than he had the entire evening with Mindy. "You're the one who said you knew all about me," he went on shortly. "You knew what I needed. You knew exactly how to find it."

"And I did!" she insisted angrily. "But I can see now I wasted my time. You're so stubborn, so sure of what you want, that it doesn't matter what I do. You're not going to be happy with anyone I find for you, are you?"

"No," he answered. "I'm not."

Cassie released a hissing breath through her teeth and turned her back on him.

Shane saw the square set of her small shoulders, the angry tilt of her head, and the irritation he had felt evaporated into tenderness, into desire, into no small measure of frustration. He let the cat slip from his arms and took a step toward her.

"Cassie," he said gently, but she didn't turn around. He took a breath and forced his voice to remain reasonable, even though all he really wanted to do was whirl her around and kiss the anger from her face. "All right, look. I didn't mean to criticize your job. Maybe Mindy was perfect for me. Okay, she was perfect. She was pleasant and she was easy to talk to and we had a lot in common." He saw her shoulders relax a little, and he went on, "But all that isn't going to make something happen that just isn't *there*. Do you know what I mean?"

"No, I don't know what you mean!" She turned around, frustration explicit in her voice and in her tight, dismissive gesture. But inside there was still that exultant little voice echoing, *Nothing happened. Nothing happened...* "You just got finished saying she was perfect, and I told you she was perfect. What did you *expect*, for heaven's sake?"

"Some spark, some chemistry."

"Oh, for the love of—! I thought you were serious. I thought you wanted someone you could spend the rest of your life with. You can't build a lifetime on chemistry!"

"No," he replied calmly, "but it's a good place to start."

Cassie looked at him, and all she could think about was the chemistry that had flared between them when they had touched, the taste of his lips, the roar of her pulse... "That's ridiculous," she said abruptly. But she wasn't quite sure who she was addressing—herself or him. And her heart was still beating much too fast.

"Cassie, look." He took another step toward her. "All I'm saying is—well, okay, maybe Mindy is perfect. But did you ever think there might be more than one perfect woman for every man?"

Cassie hesitated. She hadn't considered that. To go through all this again, to start over...

"I suppose," she admitted reluctantly. "Sometimes it does take more than one introduction. It often does, as a matter of fact. I even told you that from the beginning, didn't I?'' She couldn't muster much enthusiasm as she looked at him. ''I guess I could start looking...''

''You don't have to.''

''What?''

''I said you don't have to look. I've already found her.''

Cassie felt her heart sink to the floor. ''What?'' she repeated numbly.

''You,'' Shane said simply. ''It's you, Cassie, and I don't have to look anymore.''

The room wasn't spinning, Cassie assured herself. It was merely her head. She couldn't believe what she'd heard. The words kept echoing and she still couldn't believe it. It was her! Shane wanted her! A spiral of jubilation soared through her, and she wanted to cry out, to run to him and fling her arms around him, but the only sound that passed her lips was a stifled gasp. Her feet were rooted to the spot.

Shane's eyes were bright with questions yet intense with determination as they searched hers. He spoke quickly, as though to forestall her protest. ''Look, I know this wasn't supposed to happen, and you're going to give me a dozen reasons why it can't, but it doesn't matter. Cassie...''

He caught her upper arms gently in his and bent over her. His eyes were still searching, but deep with intensity, and his expression was set with determination. ''Cassie,'' he said again quietly. ''It's like you're inside my skin, like everything I say or do or feel is because of you and I can't concentrate on anything else except you. All the time I was with this other woman I was seeing you. Every time she spoke it was your voice I heard, and I *missed* you, Cassie. I don't want anyone else. I want you.''

His mouth covered hers and she responded helplessly, joyfully. Inside there was a voice that pleaded, *This can't be happening, it isn't right, it will never work, it simply can't be...*. But his kiss consumed her, searing her skin, weakening her muscles, blotting out reason. For one timeless, dizzying moment she lost herself in him and everything was right, nothing else mattered, and that was her gift to herself.

His hand caressed her back and her waist and slipped around to cup her left breast. Her knees went weak. His lips trailed kisses down her neck and a shiver of heat went from the darting motion of his tongue to the base of her spine. She moaned and strived for reason. ''Shane, don't... This isn't...''

''I can feel your heart beating,'' he murmured. His fingers cupped the shape of her breast. ''Cassie, tell me you don't want this.''

She made a genuine effort to twist away and looked up at him helplessly. ''We can't... get carried away by the moment. It's what I've always said, where people always make their mistake. Shane, you know this isn't right.''

''You know you don't mean that.''

No, she didn't mean it. Everything in her heart screamed she didn't mean it, but her head was equally insistent in shouting danger warnings, and in the end it was her body that saved her. Shane started to draw her close again, secure against his chest, and her muscles wanted to melt against him. But in the next moment she wrenched abruptly away, burying her face in her hands as she was overcome by a violent fit of sneezing.

"Cassie?"

He reached for her in alarm, but she waved him away, stumbling toward the coffee table and a box of tissues. She didn't know whether to laugh or cry, and between fits of sneezing she supposed she did a little of both. "Do you see?" she gasped at last. She snatched up a handful of tissues and sent the box tumbling to the floor. "Not only do we have nothing in common—" she sneezed again "—but I'm allergic to you!"

"What?" Outrage and astonishment were stamped on his face, but concern etched its way into his eyes as he came toward her. "Cassie, are you all right?"

She flung up a hand to ward him off. "No! Stay away from me." Her voice was hoarse as she buried her lower face in the wad of tissues, staving off another attack of sneezing. "Cat hair," she gasped. "You've got cat hair all over your jacket!"

Now his face registered incredulity, slowly mixed with amusement. "You're allergic to cats?"

She nodded mutely, lifting her glasses to wipe her streaming eyes as she sank onto the sofa. Shane collapsed into the chair across from her. She couldn't see his expression, but she knew his eyes were laughing. She wanted to laugh, too, but she was too miserable.

"Cassie," he said softly, and sure enough, she could hear the chuckling undertone in his voice. "You're one in a million."

Cassie covered her hot face with the tissues and said nothing. At length the sniffles abated. Slowly she lowered the tissues and looked up at Shane wretchedly, staring at him. "What are you doing?" she croaked.

He had removed his jacket and vest. Now he was standing and slowly unbuttoning his shirt. "Taking care of your allergy," he explained simply.

She didn't need her glasses to see the lean expanse of tanned chest that was gradually uncovered, the firm pectoral muscles she remembered so well, the masculine pattern of dark hair. There was a tightness in her chest and a dryness in her throat that had nothing to do with an allergic reaction as she watched him tug the wrinkled tails of his shirt from his pants, then let the garment slip to the floor.

He knelt on one knee beside her on the sofa, took her glasses from her limp fingers and set them aside. Cassie wanted to say something; she knew she should get up and move away, put an end to this. But when she lifted her hand to push him away, her fingers caressed the firm musculature of his chest instead, and the only sound that left her lips was a soft sigh. *One night, Cassie,* she thought as his lips touched the curve of her neck. *You can let go for one night....*

And, in truth, she had no choice. Long-forgotten feelings surged to life beneath the touch of Shane's fingers, the brush of his lips. Her spine seemed to melt into the curve of the sofa as he pressed a deep kiss against her throat, and a rush of helpless, dizzying sensation flooded her limbs. She sank back into the welcoming softness of the cushions and entwined her fingers in his hair as she turned her mouth to his. She tasted him greedily, her tongue playing against his in a wild mating dance.

She could feel the warmth of his chest against her breasts and the smoothness of his back beneath her fingers. Her hands traced the flexing shape of his biceps as he slipped his hands beneath her, pressing her closer. Instinctively she arched against him and felt the heat and hardness of his pelvis. He drew in a breath, and the expansion of his chest against her breasts sent ripples of sensation through her.

She raised one knee to press against his hip, and his hand followed an upward motion along her thigh, pushing aside the soft material of her nightshirt and robe until her torso was bare against him. She lifted herself a little, and he tugged her clothing over her head and then his hand was caressing her abdomen as his mouth covered her breast. A rush of moist urgency gathered between her legs, and she moaned, pressing herself against him.

The material of his trousers was scratchy against her heated, overly sensitized skin. She opened her mouth against the salty-clean taste of his shoulder and moved her hands down his back and then around, fumbling with the waistband of his trousers. He slipped his hand between their bodies to assist, and she could hear his breathing, the pounding of their separate heartbeats. In a moment he was naked against her, his strong thighs between hers, and in a single, suspended breath he slid into her, a melding of heat and sensation and a promise that had only begun.

She wound her arms around him and held him close, filled with him, absorbing him, awash in the wonder of him. His fingers stroked her eyelids. His face was hot and damp against hers. His heartbeat was wild, his breathing unsteady. And she was a part of all that was him.

"Ah, Cassie," he whispered against her cheek. "Don't you know I adore you? How can you say this is wrong?"

She couldn't remember. This was Shane, who made her laugh and made her angry, who astonished her and touched things within her she had never even guessed at before. It was Shane, whom she knew better than anyone else in the world and who was perfectly wrong for her... but nothing had ever felt so perfectly right.

The rhythms of nature overtook them, slow and sweet, then fast and urgent, propelling them and commanding them until fulfillment broke in cascades and swept them along, above and beyond themselves, no longer two but one. They held each other for a long time, reluctant to part, dazed in the glow of what they had shared. They didn't speak, not even to murmur endearments, for they didn't have to. It was enough to know what they had discovered.

Even afterward, when Cassie led Shane to her bed and they made love again, slowly and thoroughly with exquisite attention to every detail, she didn't allow the threads of rationality to intrude into their world. The magic lingered and expanded, and as long as it lasted she had no regrets.

Eight

Shane awoke to the caress of a feminine hand on his shoulder and a warmth that spread through him like liquid sunshine. He turned and saw Cassie's face, her smile soft and sleepy, her hair tousled, her cheeks pink with the remnants of sleep, and he couldn't believe that he had ever imagined waking up to any other face. He couldn't believe that anything could ever be as perfect as the way he felt this morning, looking at her.

"I have to go to work," she murmured.

"Why?" He pulled her close and flung one leg across her hips, trapping her against him. "Your most important client is right here."

Cassie laughed huskily and pressed her lips against his shoulder. "I can't argue with that."

His hand drifted over the contours of her body, curves and planes that were as familiar to him as his own, yet were still unique and exciting. The small firm breasts that filled his palms so perfectly, the fragile ribs and slim indentation of her waist, the sharp jut of her hipbone, the slender thighs... she fit against him as though she were designed for him, inch for inch, ounce for ounce. She was Cassie, and she was his.

Merely thinking of her made his heart pound in his ears; touching her sent tendrils of flame through his senses. She smiled in awareness of his body's changes and instinctively shifted her position. Wordlessly they molded themselves together, one a part of the other, just as it had always been meant to be.

Their lovemaking was lazy and luxuriant, and in a distant part of his mind Shane imagined hundreds of mornings like this, thousands. Endlessly discovering each other, reveling in each other, sharing each other forever. This was what he had been searching for all his life. How could he not have recognized it from the start?

Afterward they lay together quietly, their fingers entwined, and the slim line of sunshine that filtered through a crack in the drapes slowly moved higher and higher across the bed. Cassie thought distantly, *Daylight. How did it come so soon?* She wanted to close her eyes and pretend she had never seen morning.

"You're the best thing that ever happened to me," she whispered to Shane.

His fingers tightened on hers, and he kissed her tousled hair. "You're the only thing that's ever happened to me."

She closed her eyes against the brief, choking wash of emotion. How wonderful he was. How beautiful it had been being with him. And how badly she wanted to go on pretending, for just a little while, that this was as lovely and uncomplicated and right as it seemed at that moment.

"Do you know the only thing I'd rather do than this right now?" he asked after a while.

She glanced up at him. It was getting late. "Take a shower?" she suggested.

"Have breakfast." He glanced at her uncertainly. "I don't suppose you cook, do you?"

Cassie forced a smile, but it was a little wistful, and the glow that had sustained her through the night was fading before the harsh light of day. "Shane, I need to tell you something."

"No problem," he responded agreeably. He kissed her quickly and swung his feet onto the floor. "I'll just bet you're the type who keeps a whole stack of frozen waffles in the freezer, and it just so happens I've almost mastered frozen waffles. Just to show you how liberated I can be, I'll do breakfast."

She laughed, but even that sounded strained. She sat up to touch his arm as he fastened his pants. "Forget the waffles for a minute. This is kind of important. And awkward."

His expression softened with concern as he sat beside her on the bed, reaching for her hand. "Sure, honey, what is it?"

But Cassie didn't feel right holding his hand while she said this; neither did it seem appropriate to be naked. She extracted her robe from the tangled covers and pulled it over her shoulders, turning away from him as she flipped her hair out of her collar.

"Well, it's just that...I have a confession to make." She pretended to be busy belting and smoothing the folds of her robe and didn't look at him. "That day when you came into the office...things hadn't been going so well. The money I was going to get from you would have saved my business." And then she made herself look at him, though it took all her courage. "I never would have accepted your case otherwise. And now I feel—well, a little weird about the whole thing. I just didn't want you to find out from someone else and think that I...that I..."

She didn't know quite how to finish, but he supplied the words for her. "Would go to any lengths to keep the customer happy?"

Cassie flushed and started to turn away, but he caught her chin in his fingers. The twinkle in his eye immediately reassured her. "The only thing I'm sorry about," he told her, "is that you didn't go to these lengths sooner."

Cassie pulled her face away reluctantly. "Come on, Shane. This is serious."

"Okay, I'm sorry. I know it is." Immediately he assumed a thoughtful expression. "And I'm sorry to hear your business is in trouble. It looks like there's only one thing for you to do."

"What's that?"

"Marry me."

She laughed, but the sound got caught in her throat. "Right. That's one way to avoid a breach of contract, isn't it?" She started to get up.

"Cassie, I mean it." His voice was very sober and his fingers closed lightly around her arm. "I want you to marry me."

A chill went down Cassie's spine as she turned to look at him. He was serious. Of course he was serious. Why hadn't she seen this coming? No, the trouble was that she had seen this coming, she had known it would happen and she had done nothing to stop it. She tried to keep her voice light as she replied, "Don't be silly, Shane. I can't marry you."

Shane felt his own muscles tighten as Cassie got out of bed, walked over to the window and opened the drapes. The room was flooded with harsh morning light. "Why not?" he asked very reasonably.

"Because it wouldn't work, that's why. Because we're perfectly wrong for each other, we have nothing in common, we wouldn't last a month and we'd make each other miserable. Have you seen my glasses?"

"They're in the other room." Shane sat very still, measuring out the seconds by the beat of his heart as Cassie left the room in search of her glasses. He told himself he wasn't surprised. Why should he be surprised? It was just that, after last night, he had thought...

"Found them!" she called. She returned to the bedroom and began rummaging through a drawer. Her movements were overly energetic, jerky and false. "I wish you'd look at the time. Emma will have the sheriff out. I've really got to get moving. Here—"

"I'm in love with you, Cassie," Shane said.

Cassie stopped, a bundle of underwear clutched in her hand, and let the words go through her like tiny arrows ... arrows bathed in honey and tipped with poison. The muscles of her stomach clenched, and for a moment she couldn't get her breath. She turned to him, and it took all her strength to keep from running into his arms. "I'm in love with you, too, Shane," she whispered brokenly.

She saw joy cross his face as he started to rise, and she squared her shoulders and forced resolution into her voice as she added steadily, "And that's exactly why this has to stop."

For a moment nothing registered within Shane except incredulity. And then his careful pretense of control snapped. He leaped to his feet and exclaimed with exaggerated sarcasm, "I see! How stupid of me." He paced a few steps away from her and turned abruptly. "We're in love with each other, so naturally we can't get married! It makes perfect sense now. Thank you for explaining that."

"Shane, don't—"

"All right, I won't, if you'll be good enough to explain one more thing to me." He took an angry step toward her and gestured at the bed. "What was last night, then? Just another dress rehearsal? An *audition*?"

The hurt and betrayal in his eyes went through her like a knife. She pressed a hand against her breastbone as though to subdue it, but somehow managed to keep her voice even as she replied, "Last night was two people who wanted to make love making love. It was beautiful and I'm glad but—"

"But what? Now it's over? That's it? Just walk away?"

"Don't tell me you've never left a woman the morning after before!"

"Not like this! Damn it, Cassie. Not like this!" He thrust his fingers through his hair, seeking calm, or failing that, at least a calmer tone of voice. He found neither. "You know this wasn't just a one-night stand for me. You know what I wanted—"

"Yes, I know! You were in the mood to get married and I just happened to be available, so you thought you'd marry me! Well, I'm not available and I'm not going to marry you, Shane!"

"Why not?" he demanded.

It was so much easier to feel anger than the awful, crushing pain that bore down on her each time she looked into his eyes. It was so much easier to be aggressive than defensive, and anger was the best defense against her own weakness. She turned on him harshly.

"Have you ever been to Rome?" she demanded.

"Italy?" He seemed taken aback. "No."

"Well, I have. And I liked it. And do you know what else? I'd like to go again. Would you?"

"No, I—"

"I'd like to go to Greece, too, and this winter my parents have invited me to go on a Caribbean cruise. How do you feel about ships, Shane?"

"I don't see what this has to do with—"

"Do you belong to the country club?" she pursued ruthlessly. "I do. You hate formal dances, don't you? I love them. Do you play golf? Tennis? What do you expect us to *do* together?"

"Cassie, stop this—"

"No!" She cried. "No, because don't you see that's just the tip of the iceberg. Those aren't even the things that matter! You grew up in an orphanage filled with children and I was a spoiled only child. You've spent your life in the wilderness and I've spent mine in the city. You barely finished high school and I was reading Chaucer when I was twelve. You want a wife. I want a career. You want a homemaker and I have to hire a maid service twice a month just to keep this apartment straight! You want someone to commit to for the rest of your life and I—"

"You're afraid," he said softly.

A very strange, horribly remote look had come into his eyes, and it chilled Cassie's soul. She stopped in midbreath.

"That's what this is all about, isn't it?" he said. His voice was quiet and matter-of-fact, and he looked at her as though he had never seen her before. "It's all very easy and safe for you to arrange other people's lives, but when it comes to your own, you back away." He shook his head, and now his eyes were touched with a trace of pity. "I guess maybe you're right. You're not what I need after all."

He turned and went into the living room, and Cassie heard him gathering up his clothes. She leaned against the wall, her arms crossed on her stomach, and fought down the burning knot in her throat. After a while she heard the front door close softly behind him, and she sank to the floor and let the tears come.

Cassie went through the rest of the week in a stupor. Over and over she berated herself for ever having let things go so far with Shane. She had known such an involvement could only lead to disaster. She was supposed to be reasonable, so logical and thoughtful about everything, completely in control. Yet for one reckless moment she had cast control and reason and all her hard-earned knowledge aside for the sake of that giddy, irresponsible, dangerously seductive sensation commonly known as love, and she deserved what had happened. She deserved worse, for she had known better. But Shane didn't deserve it. He hadn't bargained for any of this.

Yet what else could she have done? He had left her no choice. Marriage. She had never even thought about marriage, not for herself, not to him. Marriage meant forever, sacrifice, compromise, devotion. Shane deserved a woman who could give him all those things and more. He would never be happy with her. She was nothing like the woman he wanted, the woman he needed. She had done the right thing in turning him down. She had done the only possible thing, and surely one day they would both be grateful she had.

Then why did it hurt so much?

Mindy Howard called to say she had never met a man she liked more than Shane Bartlett and did Cassie think he would think she was pushy if she called and asked him to go camping in the mountains next weekend? Cassie had to put her on hold while she composed herself enough to tell Mindy that it might be too soon for a camping trip and Cassie would get back to her later. She felt like a hypocrite and a charlatan when she hung up.

Every day she expected to hear from Shane. Her mood swung wildly from desperate hope to dark dread, and when nothing happened—not a phone call, not a knock on the door, not a note on her desk—she settled into a state of quiet despondency that clung about her like a shroud. She had never expected him to just walk away and not contact her again. At the very least they had the shreds of a business relationship to resolve. They should be able to sit down and talk about things like adults. They couldn't just leave things in midair, could they? What did he expect her to do?

"Do you think he could sue us?" she worried out loud to Emma. There had been no point in trying to keep the story—or at least as much of it as she could bear to tell—from the older woman. Since Cassie's mother had moved to Florida, Emma had stepped into the surrogate role, and she took her job seriously. She never would have let Cassie get away with a secret like this.

"It would be an interesting lawsuit," Emma speculated, and Cassie shivered.

"I guess the best thing to do," Cassie said, rubbing her arms anxiously, "is to give him his money back as soon as we can."

"That won't be soon."

Cassie nodded bleakly. "I know."

Emma reached across the desk and patted Cassie's hand, her face filled with concern and sympathy. "Honey, are you sure you did the right thing? Don't you feel anything for the man?"

"I feel everything for him," Cassie confessed, leaning her head back tiredly, "but you know that's not enough. Our compatibility charts don't even touch. Our incompatibility quotient is off the scale. Even he would be the first to admit I'm not the kind of woman he's attracted to.''

"But he asked you to marry him." When Cassie started to object, Emma lifted her hand and went on, "Honey, I've never pretended to know anything about your charts and formulas, and I'll be the last one to try to tell you how to run your life. All I know is that when your mother formed this social club she did so without benefit of forms or statistics and nobody ever complained. She relied on what was in here." Emma tapped her chest lightly. "And she let everyone else do the same. She knew that when the right people found each other the time for thinking about it was over. All you could do was just step back and let it happen. Don't you think life would be easier if you did the same?"

Cassie shook her head, wishing it could be that simple. "Things are different today, Emma. People are different. Commitment seems to mean something different. I don't know. All I know is that I just can't afford to take chances."

Emma smiled. "Men and women have been doing that since the beginning of time. Why should you be any different?"

Cassie was silent for a moment. "Shane said...I'm afraid. Of marriage, of permanence. Maybe he's right in a way. But it's not that I'm afraid of commitment. It's just that I don't like uncertainties. And Shane just doesn't...fit the formula."

Emma looked sadly at her, then stood. "If it will make you feel better, I'll call him next week and find out what we should do about his account."

Cassie smiled weakly in assent.

But on Monday morning she received Shane Bartlett's personality profile form in the mail: concise, mechanical, complete in every detail, and as cold and impersonal as stone. There was no longer any doubt in Cassie's mind about where their relationship stood.

She went home that night and cried until her eyes were so swollen that she couldn't see, then she resolved to put him out of her mind.

That, of course, was easier said than done.

When Cassie came into work the next morning, Emma was on the phone. There was a worried frown on her face and her voice was low. "I know you told me he was stubborn, and Lord knows, so is she, but this is the biggest mess I've ever seen. You'd think two halfway grown-up people could—"

Suddenly Emma saw Cassie and stopped with a guilty expression on her face. She murmured, "Hold on a minute," and put the party on hold. Then she smiled at Cassie. "There's a Karen Doyle in your office. Here's her form."

Cassie took the form and didn't even pause to wonder who was on the line. Emma's personal life—unlike the personal lives of everyone else in Dallas—was none of her concern.

The young woman in her office was blond, well-groomed and attractive, and she greeted Cassie with just the right amount of warmth tempered with reserve. Her figure was very nearly perfect, her makeup skillfully designed to look like natural beauty, her hair almost waist-length. She was soft-spoken and composed, and Cassie disliked her on sight.

She couldn't say exactly what it was about the young woman that set her nerves on edge, unless it was a purely female reaction to someone who was far more . . . well, female—than she. Cassie sat down and placed Karen Doyle's form on her desk next to Shane's, and then she knew exactly why the other woman made the hair on the back of her neck bristle. Here, sitting across from her, was the woman Shane had described when he first came into her office nearly a month ago.

A close comparison of the charts and the personal interview only confirmed her suspicions. Karen Doyle was twenty-two years old. She had been working in public relations but was really more of a homebody. She confessed with a laugh that all she really wanted to do was find a nice man and settle down to raise a family. Her father had been in real estate. She drove a BMW and owned a town house in one of the exclusive suburbs of Dallas, so it was obvious money was not her prime objective in seeking a man. She didn't claim to be very well-read or particularly sophisticated. She did volunteer work at a day-care center in her spare time. She didn't like parties or bars and had a hard time meeting single men. She had never been married.

Just for the hell of it, Cassie asked her what her favorite food was. "Rocky road ice cream," Karen laughingly replied.

The woman had a gorgeous tan that spoke of many hours by the pool. She loved to cook. She had a neat, orderly personality that would adapt itself well to homemaking. She had absolutely no ambition. She was perfect for Shane. She was so damn perfect that Cassie wanted to crumple up the profile form and fling it in the other woman's face. Instead, Cassie smiled politely, thanked Karen for coming in and told her she would be in touch.

She spent the rest of the afternoon comparing the two forms, making charts and taking notes. Every result only sent her deeper into despair. Once she had told Shane he couldn't just order a woman the way he could a hamburger at a restaurant. She might now have to revise that opinion. Karen Doyle was everything Shane said he wanted—tailor-made, custom-fitted, precise in every detail. That little voice kept whispering over and over in the back of Cassie's mind *But I don't like her!* Repeatedly she ignored it. Of course Cassie didn't like her; Cassie had known from the beginning that she wouldn't have anything at all in common with the kind of woman Shane was interested in.

Karen Doyle was gorgeous, unaffected, a little bit lazy and not too bright. She liked children and cooking and keeping house. She was the kind of woman who could dedicate herself completely to a man for the rest of her life without regret and count herself lucky to be able to do so. She could give Shane what he wanted.

The more Cassie studied the situation, the angrier she became—at Shane, at herself, at the impossibility of the situation that had brought them together. *He* had sent in the form, hadn't he? He had made it clear exactly what he expected from her—business as usual.

If there had been anything left at all of the feelings he so passionately professed for her, he would have called. He would have come to her. He would have tried to talk to her at least one more time. But, no, Shane Bartlett always knew what he wanted. And he wanted a wife.

At the end of the day Cassie picked up both files and dropped them on Emma's desk on her way out. Her eyes were hard, her jaw set. "Give Mr. Bartlett a call, will you?" she said diffidently. "Tell him we have someone for him to meet."

In the past ten days Shane had carried tiles, mixed concrete, driven nails and twisted wrenches. Today he was standing in the foyer, stripped to the waist in the summer heat, applying paint to the walls with aggressive, half-attentive motions. Consequently there was at least as much paint on him as on the walls, but he didn't care. All he wanted was something to do.

"I hope you're not getting union wages," said a familiar voice behind him, "because that's a pretty poor job of painting you're doing there, boy."

Shane glanced over his shoulder at Jack, distracted. "Doesn't matter. They're going to wallpaper over it, anyway."

"Whoa!" Jack stepped back as Shane slapped the paintbrush against the wall again. "Are they going to wallpaper my suit, too?"

"Sorry." Shane dropped the brush into the can and reached for a rag to dry his hands. He managed a small grin. "I never thought I'd see the day when I'd pick up a tool of any kind again, but lately I just can't seem to find enough to do. Maybe Cassie was right. Maybe I wasn't meant to just sit in the sun and do nothing." His voice fell as he concentrated his attention on meticulously scraping the paint from his nails. "Maybe she was right about a lot of things."

Jack observed him in silence for a moment, then he asked, "How's it going?"

"Oh...great." Shane gestured around the house. "Wallpaper's coming tomorrow, then the carpet. The foreman says they'll finish on schedule if I'll stop helping."

"That's not what I mean," Jack said quietly.

"Yeah, I know." Shane tossed the rag aside and sat down on an overturned paint can. "All this—" he nodded at the foyer and beyond "—is great, but it just doesn't seem as important as I thought it would. And I'll tell you the truth." Again he managed a weak smile. "I'm about to wear myself out trying to find things to do."

"That's what a woman'll do to you," Jack agreed sagely.

Shane ran his fingers through his hair, leaving white streaks and specks. "I don't sleep, I don't eat, I'm working myself to death... If I had known it was going to be like this, I would've stayed in Alaska."

"Have you heard from her?"

"Cassie?" Even saying the name made his heart jump a little, and his skin tightened. He shook his head. "Not her. Emma. She's arranged another date for me. Can you believe that? Hell, I only sent in that form so that Cassie would call me. I'm supposed to meet the girl tonight."

Jack's voice was incredulous. "And you're going to do it?"

Shane shrugged. At first he'd been so hurt he couldn't think straight, then he'd been angry, and that hadn't helped his thinking, either. It was during the angry period that he filled out the form, giving the answers he knew Cassie would most hate to hear, and sent it in. Since Emma had called he'd felt like an automaton, keeping his hands busy while his mind was on hold and his heart was stifled somewhere in his chest, almost too defeated to beat. No, he didn't want to spend another evening with another perfect woman. No, he didn't want to sit across the table from a buxom blonde while a vivacious redhead haunted the back of his mind. But lately it seemed easier to follow the course of least resistance, and he didn't know what else to do.

Cassie didn't want him. She'd made that plain.

"Cassie's a smart woman," he said. "She's been right about a lot of things. Maybe she does know what I need better than I do. Maybe I should just let her do her job."

"Hellfire and damnation, boy!" Jack swept off his hat and slapped it against his thigh with a suddenness that startled Shane. "Since when in this world do you ever let anybody tell you what you want?"

Shane was jolted into self-defense. "Well, she ought to know what *she* wants, shouldn't she? And it's not me."

Jack fixed him with a piercing stare. "You know what the trouble with you and Miss Cassie is, don't you? You're two of a kind, both so set in your ways you won't give each other an inch. She's just in the habit, that's all—in the habit of doing for other folks and not herself, of doing it all a certain way and not making room for change. She just needs somebody to give her a little push. Just like me and—"

He stopped, and Shane glanced up at him shrewdly. "Emma?"

Jack cleared his throat and a faint flush of color stained his cheeks. He put his hat back on his head. "What do you know about that?" he demanded gruffly.

"Nothing." Shane tried to suppress a smile. "Just that you do an awful lot of talking about flying to Vegas and checking out the clubs, but you spend your evenings over at her house playing cards. It doesn't take much to put two and two together."

Jack looked at him severely for a moment, and then a small, embarrassed smile tugged at his lips. "Yeah, all right, you got me there. But let's just keep this between you and me, okay? No point in making a production about it."

"Why not?" Shane asked curiously. "After all these years, what's keeping you two apart?"

"Oh, hell, I don't know." Jack scrubbed the back of his neck with his hand. "Habit, like I said. You get used to a certain way and it's hard to change. And then there's Miss Cassie." He grinned. "She says we're all wrong for each other, and she's the expert. It's kind of hard to ignore a thing like that. I mean, with all that scientific evidence hanging over your head."

Shane knew Jack was kidding, but his words registered in Shane's head with the click of a puzzle piece falling into place. "Yeah," he said slowly. "Yeah, I guess it would be hard to ignore something like that...especially if you're the expert and you spent all your life proving that's just what you were—an expert." He looked up at Jack with sudden understanding. "Even if you wanted to you couldn't admit you were wrong, could you?"

Jack clearly didn't know what his friend was getting at. Shane stood suddenly and dug into his jeans pocket. "Listen, Jack, will you do me a favor? Here's the information on that girl I'm supposed to meet tonight. Will you go to the Fairmont in my place? Just give her dinner and take her home, tell her whatever you want—"

"What?" Jack stared at the paper in his hand. "Why me? Why don't you—"

"Because," Shane explained impatiently, "she's coming in from Bridgeport and it's too late to call her now. You'll do this for me, won't you, Jack? Unless—" he hesitated "—you think it'll mess up things between you and Emma. I wouldn't want to cause any trouble."

Jack glanced at the paper in his hand, then at Shane. "Is it for love?"

"Yes," Shane said without hesitation. "It is."

Jack smiled. "Then Emma won't mind."

Shane slapped him on the back gratefully, then hurried back to the trailer to wash up and change.

Nine

Cassie had sworn she wouldn't spend another night like the last one. Shane was on a date with his perfect match and she was pacing the floor, checking her watch, tearing herself apart inside. She was *not* going to do this.

She took a deep breath, sat down on the sofa and picked up a magazine, idly flipping the pages. She didn't know what she was so upset about. She had done her job, that was all. What was she supposed to do?

But pictures kept running through the back of her mind, and she couldn't ignore them. The view from Shane's bedroom, overlooking a flower garden that hadn't been planted yet. Herself, coming down a long staircase in a white dress and train, emerging into a foyer filled with flowers and smiling guests. A great room filled with chintz furniture and Navaho pottery and the two of them standing with their arms around each other's waists, watching the sunset. Deliberately she blacked out the picture.

Fluffy jumped up on the sofa and arched against Cassie's arm, purring loudly. Cassie absently drew the cat into her lap. Karen Doyle was a perfectly nice young lady and Shane was a grown-up man. They were both capable of making up their minds about each other. It was out of Cassie's hands.

Karen Doyle was a vapid, mindless mantrap, and Shane would be knocked off his feet by her. "So they can eat rocky road ice cream and grow fat together," she muttered. Fluffy rubbed against her face and she sneezed.

The picture in her mind resurfaced, and this time a child was playing on the front lawn, tossing a tennis ball for a brown-and-white dog that had once been a puppy. The child was a boy, with auburn hair and warm brown eyes. Cassie felt a catch in her chest.

Once she had told Shane he didn't know himself well enough to know what he wanted. Was it possible that theory worked both ways? How could she have know what she wanted until someone offered it to her? She couldn't get the picture of that little boy playing on the lawn out of her mind. She could still feel Shane's arm around her waist and her head on his shoulder, and years seemed to roll forward on the screen of her vision, good years and bad years, until it was grandchildren who played on that lawn....

Oh, God, she thought, burying her face in a tissue. *Why did I do this? I don't want Shane to find another woman. I don't want him to be with any woman ex-*

*cept me. How could I have been so stupid? Why did I
do this?*

She raised her face and looked at the telephone. Two
swift strides took her to it and she punched out the
number. It rang and rang, and her heart beat louder
with each ring. Finally she let the receiver fall back into
the cradle. Too late. He had already left.

She stood there, stared at the telephone and tried to
tell herself it was for the best. What would she say to
him, anyway? But it wasn't for the best. And she knew
what she'd say: that she loved him and she was sorry
and nothing else mattered and she'd been a fool not to
see that before. But how could she have known it when
she had never loved anyone before? How could she
know what havoc love could wreak with logic, how it
could turn reason inside out and refuse to comply with
the formulas she had relied on all her life? Love was a
law unto itself. How could anyone understand that
until it happened?

The sound of the doorbell jolted her nerves, and she
tripped over the cat in her rush to answer it. Her heart
was beating wildly and her breathing was labored as she
flung open the door, almost as though she had known
who would be standing there.

And she was right. He was wearing jeans, a cotton
shirt and vest, a Stetson hat and those wonderful, an-
cient, battered boots. His jaw was knotted and his eyes
were stern and there were specks of paint on his hands
and in his hair. He was the most beautiful sight Cassie
had ever seen.

He strode through the door and tossed his hat onto
the chair. ''Why do you keep the cat?'' he demanded
abruptly.

Cassie took a small step backward, blinking at him. "Wh-what?"

"The cat," he repeated. "You're allergic to it. Why do you keep it?"

Cassie hesitated, trying to orient herself. Her heartbeat was still racing and her limbs were quivering and all she could think of was that he was here, not with Karen, but with her. He was here....

"Be-because," she managed distractedly, "because Fluffy can't help being a cat. And I love her."

"Cassie." His eyes softened with tenderness as he took a step toward her. "Can't you keep me for the same reason? I love you. And I can't help being me."

With a muffled cry she flung herself into his arms. Her lips found his, and whatever words she might have said were forgotten. She hardly knew when he swept her into his arms and carried her to the bedroom. Nor was she aware of their clothes falling away. The room was lit only by the filtered streetlight from the window and glow of the lamp from the other room. His sleek, shadowed form hovered over her as she sank back against the pillows. Her hands caressed the sinewy lines of his arms and the taut indentation of his waist and her fingers tangled briefly in the hair on his chest. His arms slipped beneath her shoulders, drawing her upward, and she opened her mouth to him. His tongue invaded her mouth with a rush of liquid heat and a flare of color behind her closed eyelids. She moved against him urgently, and the kiss became only an extension of a greater, more demanding need as he slid inside her.

They moved with rhythms that were sweet and slow, then fierce and hungry, a silent harmonious communication that built in intensity with each whispered caress, each breathless kiss. The world outside with all its problems and uncertainties dissolved for Cassie, and she knew only the touch of Shane's skin against hers, the strength of his muscles surrounding her, his heat filling her. When the pinnacle of need was reached and began to shatter into ripples of cascading pleasure, she clung to him and let the joy wash through her, blinding her for a moment to everything except Shane. It was like coming home. They were together, just as it was meant to be. Just as it would always be.

There was so much still to be said, so much that remained unresolved. But lying there secure in his arms, it all seemed unimportant and far away. The only thing that mattered was that Shane was here. She had been given another chance, and this time she wasn't going to run away from what her heart demanded.

Though she didn't really care to hear the answer, after a time she felt obligated to ask, "What happened to Karen?"

His fingertips stroked a delicious pattern along her collarbone. "I gave her to Jack."

She chuckled softly, absurdly gratified. "She was perfect for you."

"Darlin', haven't you figured out by now that I don't want the perfect woman? I want you."

She propped herself on her elbows and leaned over him, her heart filled to overflowing with things she had to say, things that had needed to be said for too long. "Oh, Shane..."

The phone began to ring.

He caressed her shoulder persuasively. "Don't answer it."

For a moment she was tempted, but the persistent shrilling left her little choice. She gave him an apologetic look and turned away to answer the phone.

She listened in stunned incredulity to the frantic voice on the other end for several moments, and she didn't recall what, if any answer, she gave. She returned the receiver to its cradle and turned slowly back to Shane.

He saw the expression on her face and sat up. "Cassie? Is something wrong?"

Cassie opened her mouth to speak but had to clear her throat before the words would come out. Utter bafflement dulled her tone as she looked at him. "That was Emma. She's at the police station. Jack—and Karen—have been arrested."

The inside of the police station was as crowded and confusing as police stations are supposed to be, and despite Shane's constant reassurances that there had been some mistake, Cassie's nerves went from frazzled to shredded in the twenty minutes it took them to get someone to tell them where to find Jack. Eventually they were escorted to an interrogation room where the scene was only slightly less confusing than the one they had just left.

Emma and Jack were standing on the opposite sides of a small table, each talking louder than the other. In the middle was a rumpled, tired and bored-looking detective who had apparently given up trying to take their statements long ago.

"I still don't understand what you were doing there."

"I told you, Shane asked me to—"

"A hotel, of all places!"

"There's a restaurant there, too, you know!"

"She's thirty years younger than you, Jack!"

"What difference does that make? I wasn't—"

"Emma!" Cassie flew across the room. "What happened? What are you doing here? What's going on?"

Jack glared at Emma across the table. "I told you not to call her." He glanced at Shane and muttered, "Sorry about this."

Shane hooked his thumbs in his pockets and glanced around the room noncommittally. "How's it going, Jack?"

"Not too well, if you want to know the truth."

The detective stood just as Cassie was getting ready to grab Emma and shake some answers out of her. "Are you Cassie Averil, the owner of the service?"

Cassie turned to him quickly. "Yes. Yes, I am. Now will you please tell me what's going on?"

"And do you know a Miss Karen Doyle?"

Cassie looked quickly at Emma. "Yes, she's a client of mine. What's this all about?"

"A client, huh?" The detective looked sour. "That's one way of putting it, I guess. You paid Karen Doyle to escort Mr. Sanders for the evening?"

Cassie turned in confusion from Emma to Jack. "No, of course not. She paid me. And she wasn't supposed to go out with Jack at all. She was supposed to go out with Shane."

"You see?" Jack told the detective grumpily. "That's what I've been trying to tell you!"

"You haven't told me anything," replied the detective implacably. "All I know was that you were seen completing a financial transaction with Miss Doyle."

"I gave her carfare, for Pete's sake."

"What's going on here?" Cassie practically screamed.

The detective gave her an admonishing look. "Mr. Sanders," he replied calmly, "has been arrested on charges of pandering."

Cassie stared at Jack, and he shifted his gaze away, embarrassed.

"Miss Doyle, a known prostitute," continued the detective, "has been charged with solicitation."

Cassie felt all the breath leave her lungs.

"And you, Miss Averil," the detective added, "will most likely be brought up on charges of running an escort service unless I have evidence to the contrary, and very quickly. It's late and my shift was over half an hour ago."

Cassie groped blindly for a chair, and Jack fumbled to push one forward just before her knees gave way. The next thing she knew someone was pushing a glass of water into her hand, Emma was fanning her face furiously, and Shane was kneeling beside her. His eyes were a riot of incredulity and amusement as he accused, "A hooker? My perfect match is a *hooker*?"

Cassie slumped back weakly in the chair, and it was at that point that everything spun out of control.

Emma turned on the detective like a lioness defending its cub. "Now see what you've done! I'll have you know this young lady is from one of the finest families in this city and you dare—"

"I *told* you not to call her!" Jack said.

Shane pulled Cassie's head onto his shoulder, and it was a long time before she realized he was shaking with laughter. Cassie remembered very little after that. At some point Shane recovered himself enough to bring some semblance of order to the room. He sat down with the detective and explained everything from the beginning, and Cassie confirmed his story with a blank, stricken face and a tiny voice. Emma and Jack put aside their own differences long enough to supply the pertinent details. Karen Doyle was brought in, and although she admitted to her former profession, she swore that her relationship with Cassie was strictly legitimate and that she had genuinely left the business behind. Her apology sounded sincere as she added that all she really wanted was to find a husband.

After what seemed like an eternity to Cassie, Detective Sylby realized Cassie was innocent of any complicity and dropped the charges against Jack. Reluctantly he let Karen go, too, but with a stern warning. Shane, Cassie, Emma and Jack were left alone in the stale-smelling little room, and Cassie felt as though she had just been through a whirlwind, one she had never seen coming.

At length Shane broke the silence. "Well," he commented casually, "I guess that just goes to show you can't learn everything about a person from a form."

Everything snapped together inside of Cassie, as though his words were the focus for the entire previous nightmarish hour, and she whirled on him. "It was *your* form!" she cried furiously. "You're the one who was so certain what he wanted! All I did was match you with the woman you described and—"

Shane's eyes were twinkling. "That's what I wanted to see—the old spark in your eyes again!"

"This isn't funny, Shane! This is a disaster! You don't know—"

He took her shoulders and stilled her words with a kiss. "Ah, Cassie," he murmured, still chuckling, "never a dull moment. Life with you will never be boring. That much is sure."

Cassie rested her head against his chest and let her arms slide around his waist. After a moment she smiled, not because she saw anything funny about their situation, but because Shane was holding her in his arms and nothing had ever felt better in her life. But even that refuge couldn't completely shield her from the problems that were battering at her, and after a moment she looked at Shane anxiously.

"Oh, Shane," she said, "My business... If this gets out, my reputation—I'll be ruined!"

Shane's expression sobered. "And you can be sure it will get out. There's nothing the papers love more than a scandal like this. We're going to have to work hard to salvage something from this."

She caught her breath, searching his face. "We?'

"Of course. I figure that's part of a man's job, to help his wife when she needs it." And almost before she could register those words, he continued with the trace of an almost embarrassed grin. "I'll tell you something. You were right about my having a head for business. And the truth is, I was getting kind of tired of sitting in the sun. So maybe I could just be semiretired."

"Oh, Shane—"

He lifted a hand to silence her. Neither was aware of the interested attention they were receiving from Emma and Jack.

"That's what I really came over to tell you tonight," he said seriously. "That you were right about me—about a lot of things. I spent so long dreaming about the perfect life I was going to have that I got the fantasy all mixed up with reality and I didn't even know a good thing when I saw it. I know we're not much alike, Cassie, and we don't have anything in common, but that will be the fun of it. Don't you see? Learning about each other. So we'll fight. I like fighting, just like you said. I like doing things the hard way, and God help me if I'm wrong, but so do you. I want a woman who can talk to me, who knows things I don't, who can put me in my place when I get out of hand, who makes me laugh and makes me mad and makes every single moment worth living. Just like you do, Cassie. You were right all the time about me. It just took a little time to admit it, that's all."

Cassie folded her fingers around his lapels, smiling through a sudden film of happy tears. "I might have been right about some things, Shane," she said huskily, "but I was wrong about a lot of others. Mostly about what I wanted."

"I meant it when I said I wanted to help you in your business," he said urgently. "And you're right. I can hire a housekeeper and learn to cook."

Cassie laughed and looked up at him with sudden mischief. "You don't have to," she told him. "That's another thing I didn't tell you about myself. I'm a gourmet cook."

Shane closed his eyes, tilted his head to the heavens and murmured, "Thank you, God." Then he tightened his arms around her, laughed softly and declared, "Cassie Averil, you're a miracle. I'm glad I decided to marry you."

Cassie lifted her face to his for a kiss and said softly, "I am, too."

Emma and Jack exchanged a triumphant look. Emma folded her arms across her chest and declared, "Well, it's about time!"

And Jack added smugly, "Didn't I tell you there was nothing to worry about? All we had to do was get them together and let nature do the rest."

Cassie lifted her head from Shane's chest, staring at Emma in slow suspicion. "You—?"

Shane turned to Jack, obviously as surprised as Cassie was. "You! You're the one who sent me to her in the first place!"

"And, Emma," Cassie accused, "you were in on this from the beginning?"

"In on it? It was my idea!" And she smiled at them benignly. "I was playing matchmaker before you were born, missy. Between the two of us—" she tucked her arm through Jack's confidently, "—you never had a chance."

Shane encircled Cassie's shoulders with his arm, his eyes twinkling down at her. "Well, it looks like we've been set up. What do you think we should do about it?"

The tensions and regrets of the past week, the bizarre blurred events of the past hour, the indecision and uncertainties of Cassie's entire life, fell away in cascades of warmth as she looked into Shane's eyes. "Celebrate?" she suggested.

"Sounds like a damn fine idea to me," Jack agreed boisterously. "Let's get out of this place!"

"Just a minute." Shane held up his hand. "Now that you've got Cassie and me straightened out, don't you think the two of you ought to get some things settled between you?"

Emma suddenly seemed to realize how intimately her arm was entwined with Jack's, and started to pull away. Jack looked uncomfortable for a minute, then covered Emma's hand with his own. He cleared his throat and said, "Well, there might be a few things we could talk about."

Emma went a brilliant shade of red, but her eyes were sparkling as she responded sternly, "As long as the first thing we talk about is what business you've got going out with twenty-year-old girls."

"Now, I told you—"

Under the cover of their playful bickering, Cassie looked at Shane anxiously and protested, "Emma and Jack? But, Shane, they have nothing in common. They—" Shane laid a light, warning finger across his lips, and she lowered her eyes, abashed. "I forgot," she murmured. "Not everything can be written on a form."

Shane kissed her forehead. "You're learning."

Smiling, they walked arm in arm out into the night. Emma and Jack followed them at a much slower pace, holding hands.

* * * * *

SILHOUETTE® *Desire*™

COMING NEXT MONTH

#559 SUNSHINE—Jo Ann Algermissen
A Florida alligator farm? It was just what ad exec Rob Emery *didn't* need! But sharing the place with Angelica Franklin made life with the large lizards oh, so appealing....

#560 GUILTY SECRETS—Laura Leone
Leah McCargar sensed sexy houseguest Adam Jordan was not *all* he claimed. But before she could prove him guilty of lying, she became guilty...of love.

#561 THE HIDDEN PEARL—Celeste Hamilton
Aunt Eugenia's final match may be her toughest! Can Jonah Pendleton coax shy Maggie O'Grady into leading a life of adventure? The next book in the series *Aunt Eugenia's Treasures*.

#562 LADIES' MAN—Raye Morgan
Sensible Trish Becker knew that Mason Ames was nothing more than a good-looking womanizer! But she still couldn't stop herself from succumbing to his seductive charms.

#563 KING OF THE MOUNTAIN—Joyce Thies
Years ago Gloria Hubbard had learned that rough, tough William McCann was one untamable man. Now he was back in town...and back in her life.

#564 SCANDAL'S CHILD—Ann Major
When May's *Man of the Month* Officer Garret Cagan once again saved scandalous Noelle Martin from trouble, the Louisiana bayou wasn't the only thing steaming them up....

AVAILABLE NOW:

#553 HEAT WAVE
Jennifer Greene

#554 PRIVATE PRACTICE
Leslie Davis Guccione

#555 MATCHMAKER, MATCHMAKER
Donna Carlisle

#556 MONTANA MAN
Jessica Barkley

#557 THE PASSIONATE ACCOUNTANT
Sally Goldenbaum

#558 RULE BREAKER
Barbara Boswell

AVAILABLE NOW—

the books you've been waiting for by one of America's top romance authors!

DIANA PALMER
DUETS

Ten years ago Diana Palmer published her very first romances. Powerful and dramatic, these gripping tales of love are everything you have come to expect from Diana Palmer.

This month some of these titles are available again in DIANA PALMER DUETS—a special three-book collection. Each book has two wonderful stories plus an introduction by the author. You won't want to miss them!

Book 1
SWEET ENEMY
LOVE ON TRIAL

Book 2
STORM OVER THE LAKE
TO LOVE AND CHERISH

Book 3
IF WINTER COMES
NOW AND FOREVER

Available now at your favorite retail outlet.